blacklisted

GENA SHOWALTER

POCKET BOOKS   MTV BOOKS

New York   London   Toronto   Sydney

Pocket Books, A Division of Simon & Schuster, Inc.
1230 Avenue of the Americas
New York, NY 10020

First MTV Books/Pocket Books trade paperback edition July 2007

Designed by Carla Jayne Little

Manufactured in the United States of America

10 9 8 7 6 5 4 3 2

ISBN-13: 978-1-4165-3225-5
ISBN-10:   1-4165-3225-0

For information about special discounts for bulk purchases,
please contact Simon & Schuster Special Sales at
1-800-456-6798 or business@simonandschuster.com.

blacklisted

Also by Gena Showalter

Oh My Goth

Red Handed

This one is for my brother, Shane Tolbert,
who's often been my knight in shining armor.

Acknowledgments

Thank you to Shonna Hurt and Michelle Quine. I would be lost without you.

Prologue

Erik Trinity had a system for buying drugs.

Always during the day. Fewer Alien Investigation and Removal agents prowling the streets.

Always in the open. Less chance of being pinned in.

And always in a crowd. Even A.I.R. avoided firing when innocents were around.

He knew this because *he* was an agent. Erik winced, hating himself. How he wished the drugs were part of an undercover assignment. But they weren't. What he did was illegal.

If anyone learned of his extracurricular activities, he would spend the rest of his life in prison. But he refused to stop. He *couldn't* stop.

Too many people relied on him.

Each transaction usually took less than two seconds. He walked one direction and the seller walked in the other. As they passed, they made their switch. Cash for Onadyn. Neither slowed, neither said a word. Just *boom*. Done.

Today had been no different. He already had several vials in his jacket pocket. His part wasn't over, though. Now it was time to pass them to their new owners.

After checking for a tail and finding nothing suspicious in the laughing throng of people milling about and shopping in New Chicago's pulsing town square, he hopped a bus to the Southern District, the poor side of town. Soon polished chrome-and-glass buildings gave way to crumbling, charred red brick that hadn't seen much repair since the Human-Alien War some seventy years ago.

The streets became less crowded, and the people who occupied them less . . . clean. Both humans and Outers resided here, but Erik mainly saw Outers slumped against dilapidated walls—white-haired Arcadians, six-armed Delenseans, catlike Terans—either too sick or too weak to move.

Judging by a few frozen expressions, some were probably already dead. Erik's hands clenched at his sides. What senseless deaths. Preventable and unnecessarily cruel. They so easily could have been saved.

Scowling, he exited at his stop. Warm sunlight instantly washed over him, attracted to the black jacket, T-shirt, and jeans he wore. Inconspicuous and forgettable clothing no matter who stood around him.

He performed another perimeter check. Still nothing suspicious. *So close to being done,* he thought, his relief so potent it overshadowed his disgust. He was always on edge until the last vial was out of his possession.

Get it done. Erik kicked into motion along the urine-scented sidewalk, hands in his pockets, head slightly down. He rounded a corner and heard a pain-filled moan. *Don't stop. Don't look.* Yet his gaze zeroed in on a young girl writhing in pain.

Keep moving, one part of him said. He'd seen hundreds of aliens die like this; he'd probably see a hundred more.

Help her, the other part screamed.

He had about an hour, tops, to get the Onadyn to its new owners and catch a ride home. Otherwise, his girlfriend would wake up alone and wonder where he was. And if Cara wondered, Cara would ask questions. She was an agent, too, so she knew how to suck every little scrap of information from him—information that would destroy him.

No, he didn't have time for this. He crouched down anyway.

"Where are your parents?" he gently asked the girl.

"Dead," she managed to rasp out. Her little body jerked, the muscles spasming erratically. Her eyelids squeezed together, cutting off his view of glassy violet eyes. She rolled into a ball.

Dirt smudged her from head to toe, and he could see lice jumping in her snow-white hair. She was Arcadian, probably no more than eight years old. Agony radiated from her. More than most adults could have handled. More than *he* could have handled.

"There's no one else to take care of you?" he asked, already sensing the answer.

Her mouth floundered open and closed, but no sound emerged. She was struggling to breathe, no longer able to draw a single molecule of air into her lungs. His stomach knotted as her skin colored blue.

He didn't have an ounce of Onadyn to spare, but he couldn't leave her like this. Without the drug, which allowed certain alien species to tolerate Earth's environment, she would die exactly as the people around her had died. And if that happened, her angel face would haunt him for the rest of his life.

Damn this and damn me. He looked left, then right. No one seemed to be paying them the slightest bit of attention, so he withdrew a clear vial from his pocket. He held it to her lips and poured at least a week's salary down her throat.

He would have to buy more. Which meant lying to Cara (again) and spending money he no longer had (again).

Was it worth it?

Almost instantly, the girl's color began to return, pale cream chasing away pallid blue. Her features smoothed and her body relaxed. A contented smile slowly curled the corners of her lips.

Erik sighed. Yeah, it was worth it. Knowing she would live—at least for a little while—he pushed to his feet and walked away. He didn't look back. For once he felt like the agent he was supposed to be, rather than the despicable agent he'd become.

1

A few months later . . .

Have you ever stumbled upon a secret you wished to God you'd never learned? A dark and dangerous secret? A secret people would kill to protect?

I have.

And, yeah, I almost died for it.

My name is Camille Robins. I'm eighteen and in my last month at New Chicago High, District Eight.

It all began on a balmy Friday evening when my friend Shanel Stacy borrowed her parents' car and picked me up . . .

"I can't believe we're doing this," I said, already breathless with anticipation and nerves. I slid into the passenger seat.

"Believe it, baby," Shanel said as she buckled into the driver's side. With a few clicks of the keyboard, she programmed the Ship's address into the car's console, and we eased out of my driveway and onto the street.

Because sensors kept the car from hitting anyone or thing and because computers navigated the roads, we didn't have to steer or even keep our eyes on our surroundings. We could chat and consider all the things that might go wrong at the famous nightclub.

Get caught lying to our parents—a possibility. We'd told them we were staying the night with another friend of ours. A friend we'd invented. Get thrown out—another possibility. We weren't rich or fabulous like the usual patrons. Make fools of ourselves—the biggest possibility of all.

Neither one of us had style.

Shanel studied me, her intent gaze starting at my dark hair and stopping on my boots. Underneath, my toenails were painted blue to match my eyes. "Why do you look like you're one second away from barfing on the floorboards?"

"I'm not good at clandestine activities. You know that."

"This isn't clandestine. This is *fun*."

"Fun?" So not the word I would have used.

"Oh yeah." Shanel smiled slowly. "Fun." But a moment passed in silence and she lost her grin. Her expression became pensive. "I wish I was an Outer."

Outer. Aka alien. My face scrunched in confusion. "Why?"

"Think about it. Some of them can control humans with

their minds. I could make boys fall in love with us; I could force people to notice us; we could become *the* most popular girls at school—no, the world—with only a thought."

Sounded good in theory, but . . . I have nothing against Outers, I just don't want to be one, no matter what their powers are. They lived and walked among us, but some people still hated them and treated them as less than, well, human. I've seen them teased and taunted unmercifully. I've seen them pushed and beaten.

I wanted to be noticed, but I wanted it to be for something good.

Besides, Outers didn't look like us. Some of them had horns. Horns! And not just on their heads. Some of them had blue skin and multiple arms (ick), some of them excreted a gooey green slime (gag). Some of them changed color with their moods (okay, that wasn't so bad).

"What if those mind-controlling powers you want so badly came with a price? Like green scales and fish breath?" I asked. Yeah, some of them had those, too. "Would you still want to be an Outer?"

Shanel shuddered.

I'd take that as a no. Shanel and I were "Invisibles," not seen or heard by our school's elite, but even our socially nonexistent lives were better than those of the Outers. "So, uh, do you think he'll be there?"

She didn't have to ask who *he* was. Erik Troy. Gorgeous, delectable, mouthwatering Erik Troy. A boy who rarely glanced in my direction, despite the fact that staring at him had become my favorite hobby.

"I told you," Shanel said. "I was standing at my locker and heard Silver tell him they'd meet at the club."

Silver and Erik were best friends and the hottest boys at our school. While Erik was human, Silver was an Outer. A Morevv, one of the most beautiful races I'd ever encountered. I admit it: I wouldn't mind looking like a Morevv, with creamy skin and angelic facial features.

Truly, Silver was the only fully accepted alien I knew.

Shanel wanted him; I wanted Erik (obviously). A perfect match-up for sure: best friends hooking up with best friends. If only the boys would cooperate.

"Think Ivy will be there?" Shanel asked with a bitter edge.

"Probably not." Silver had an on-again-off-again thing with popular Ivy Lynn, a human and someone I'd always wanted to be. The two were currently *off*.

Erik, too, was a free man. But he liked his girls older—or so I'd heard. Probably because *he* looked older than the average high school boy. He was bigger, stronger, more masculine.

"Do I look okay?" I asked, my nervousness increasing.

Shanel's green gaze swept over me and she grinned. "You're like a sexy beast ready to be unleashed."

I couldn't help but return her grin. She'd always had a flare for the dramatic. "Yeah, but do I look *old*?"

"Baby, you're practically geriatric. If I didn't know you, I'd swear you were nearing thirty!"

I nodded with satisfaction. The length of my long brown hair was pulled back in a tight ponytail to highlight the ten pounds of makeup I'd spackled on, and I wore a black syn-leather brassiere top with matching skirt. It was nice to be out of my conservative school uniform and in something sexy.

"What about me?" Shanel asked, skimming her palms over her curves.

I gave her a once-over. Moonlight seeped from the car windows and surrounded her in golden light. Her skin was pale and freckled, her eyes just a bit too large. She wore a tight pink dress that totally clashed with her mass of red curls, but somehow looked great on her. "Silver's going to be drooling over you."

Squealing, she clapped and held out her arm, wrist up. "Sweet. Now, smell me."

I sniffed and my nose wrinkled. "Uh, I'm sorry to tell you this, but you smell like dirt."

"Don't be sorry. That's wonderful news! I did a little recon and learned Morevvs adore earthy scents. I rubbed mud into all my pulse points just before I picked you up."

"Diabolical." I grinned.

The buildings outside were getting taller and closer to-gether, so I knew we'd reach the club very soon. Another wave of nervousness hit me. "What if we can't get in?"

"Oh, will you stop worrying?" She ran her tongue over her lips. "You know the Ell Rollis my dad hired to work on our house? Well, I commanded him to meet us at the club. He'll get us in."

My eyes widened. Ell Rollises were a race of ugly . . . things that smelled like garbage. They were big, unnaturally strong, and once given an order they thought only of that order. Only when the task was completed did they relax. If Shanel had ordered him to get us inside the Ship, he'd get us inside by any means necessary.

Maybe Erik would ask me to dance.

The car eased to a stop and a feminine computerized voice said, "Destination arrived."

Shanel uttered another squeal of delight and punched in the code for parking. A few seconds later, the car stopped. "This is going to be the greatest night of our lives!"

A girl could hope at least. We emerged and stood outside, gazing over at the club as a warm breeze slinked around us. Made of polished silver chrome, the Ship was shaped like a round, multilayered craft with hundreds of lights circling every other tier.

Even from this distance we could hear the gyrating music, a bump, bump, grind that demanded movement. A line stretched around the building and led all the way to the opening. I searched the masses for Erik, but I didn't see any sign of his (hot) body or (sexy) blond head. Was he already inside?

"You ready?" Shanel asked me.

Breathing deeply of perfumes, sweat, and eco-friendly exhaust, I gripped Shanel's hand. "Don't leave my side, okay?"

"Don't insult me. As if I'd leave you." She glanced toward the crowd and gasped happily. "Look. There's the Ell Rollis. Come on." She leapt into motion—leaving me behind.

With a sigh, I raced after her, high heels clicking against the pavement.

The closer we came to the club, the louder the music and voices became and the more realization set in. God, I could get in so much trouble for this. I usually obeyed my parents and followed their rules exactly. Only the thought of spending time with Erik had been able to lure me to the dark side.

Shanel ground to a stop in front of the male Ell Rollis who stood at the curb. When the Outer spotted her, he nodded in greeting. He had dry, yellow skin, no nose (that I could see), and sharp lizardlike teeth. I tried not to stare.

"I wait here just like you say," he told her, his voice heavily accented.

"Thank you, John. Now, here's what I want you to do next. Create a distraction so that Camille and I can get inside that building." She pointed to the double doors. "Then, run away and hide. Okay?"

John—what a weird name for such an inhuman creature—gave another nod and stomped in the direction Shanel had pointed, pushing through the thick crowd. We followed. A few people gasped, a few growled in anger. Most smiled nervously and moved out of the way, as if their greatest wish was to please the hulking beast.

Up front, John skidded to a stop. Two burly guards waited

behind a glowing, blue laserband that stretched across the doors, preventing anyone from passing. In unison, the men crossed their hands over their massive chests.

"I will distract you now," John told them.

The two men looked at each other and laughed.

"You're ugly and you stink," one said. "Go away."

Without another word, John reached out and grabbed him by the throat, lifting him off the ground. Murmurs and gasps swept through the crowd. Scared, I backed up a step. I might have even run back to the car, but Shanel tugged me into a shadowy corner.

"Let him go, you alien scum." The guard still standing withdrew a pyre-gun from his waist and aimed it at John's chest.

Before he could fire, John knocked it against the wall and it shattered. All the while, he shook the guy he held, the man's legs nearly touching the laserband. If they did, his clothes and skin would be horribly singed.

"Turn off the laser, Turk," he commanded his friend. His features were pale—no, blue. And only getting bluer. "Turn. Off. Laser."

I gulped.

"Laser!"

With a shaky hand, Turk punched in the code. Instantly the laser faded as if it had never been there.

John grinned and dropped the now-wheezing guard. "You good boys."

Shanel jerked me past the distracted pair, past the double doors, and into the building. Just like that, we were in. I glanced backward and watched as the crowd surged forward to get inside, as well. John headed in the opposite direction, sprinting away just as he'd been ordered.

Maybe *my* parents needed to employ an Ell Rollis. But they were expensive to keep, their appetites legendary, and more and more they were being picked up and locked away by the deadly and much-feared A.I.R. because too many humans commanded them to do bad things.

Who cares about that? You're in. In!

Shanel stopped, turned toward me, and wrapped me in a hug. "Can you believe it?" she shouted happily.

I grinned, all my worries melting away. The night, it seemed, had only just begun.

2

Shanel and I stopped at the edge of the foyer and gazed at a scene we'd only been able to dream about. Until now. Smoke billowed in every direction and rock music blasted from hidden amplifiers. Pink, blue, and yellow lights swirled from the center of the dance floor, illuminating the throng of writhing, dancing people.

The walls produced holographic images of kissing couples and I had to press my lips together to keep from staring in open-mouthed awe. And jealousy.

"Where should we go?" I asked Shanel, projecting my voice over the music.

"Want to try the second level?" She pointed upward. "We can look down and see if the guys are dancing."

I nodded. We maneuvered through people and smoke and pounded up the stairs. I almost screamed when the steps began to waver, swinging slowly from side to side. My fingers curled around the rail, keeping me steady.

Moving stairs wasn't a smart thing to have in a building that served alcohol. What if someone fell? I mean, really. *Lawsuit.* My dad was an attorney and that was just the sort of thing he lived for.

When we reached the second level, the music faded to a dull screech and I realized it was because glass panels circled the entire enclosure, not only blocking sound but preventing anyone from tumbling to their death.

"I've heard about stairs like that," Shanel told me with a wide grin. "When a person has had too much to drink, it's supposed to balance their equilibrium. This is so fan-freaking-tastic!" Laughing, she flounced to the bar.

I followed her and rested my elbows on the speckled counter.

"What'll you have, miss?" the bartender immediately asked me. He was a Delensean. He had blue skin—all of his kind did—and six arms, making him able to serve multiple people at once.

"Um, uh . . ."

He tapped his fingers in impatience.

"Water, please," I finally said.

He slapped all six of his hands on the emerald-veined marble separating us. "This is a bar, human, not a bathhouse. Order a drink or leave."

"O—okay. I'll have a Mad Mec, then." That's what my mom always ordered when we went out for dinner.

When my drink arrived, a glowing red liquid in a frosted

glass, I picked it up and turned to Shanel, who was sipping some kind of orange concoction. "Mmm," she said through a sigh. "This is good."

I pretended to sip mine, letting the fiery red liquid tease (and numb) my lips. I did *not* want to get drunk and make a fool of myself in front of Erik.

"Ohmygod!" Shanel suddenly gasped out and pointed. "Silver's here. He's really here!"

"Where?" Heart hammering, I whipped around to face the direction in which she pointed. I caught the barest hint of wide shoulders and blue hair before Silver disappeared up the stairs.

"Let's go before we lose him." Shanel raced forward.

I remained close on her heels. "Did you see any sign of Erik?"

"No, sorry," she threw over her shoulder, red curls bouncing. "But he has to be here somewhere. They're never far apart."

The revolving steps didn't freak me out this time and I managed to climb them with ease. However, I was moving so quickly my drink sloshed over the rim of my glass, running down my hand. Ick. Sticky.

Shanel stopped at the top and stomped her foot. "I don't see him. Do you?"

My gaze scanned the area. There weren't many people this high up, which made my search very easy. They weren't here. "Let's go up one more level," I said, disappointed.

"Hurry."

We tread the rest of the way up the stairs and stood at the edge of the highest level. This far up, the music was barely a hum. There were quite a few people scattered about, talking and laughing, some sitting at tables, some lounging on black velvet couches.

"I see him," Shanel whispered fiercely. She gripped my forearm. "He's talking to Erik."

My mouth dried completely, leaving no hint of moisture. "Where?" I whispered just as fiercely, my gaze once again moving over the room.

"On the far couch. Sitting by the—Ohmygod, they're looking this way." She turned away from them, facing me. "Act natural. Say something funny."

"Uh—uh . . ." Suddenly my gaze connected with Erik's and I lost my breath. What should I do? What the hell should I do?

In my dreams, Erik always smiled the first moment he spied me. He always stood and approached me, wanting desperately to be near me. To touch me . . . to kiss me. In reality, his brown eyes narrowed on me; his lips thinned. In displeasure? My heart sank. Why displeasure? Did I look *that* bad?

As always, *he* looked amazing. His light hair was shaggy and hung over his forehead; the dark roots gleamed in the shadowy light. I think his hair was naturally brown, but he looked good as a blond. He had an eyebrow ring, a slightly crooked nose that had probably been broken a time or two, and sharp-as-glass cheekbones.

Out of his school uniform—the same white button-up and black slacks I had to wear—he was yummy. Right now he wore a black T-shirt and faded jeans. Both hugged him deliciously.

Shanel forced a laugh. "Oh, that's hilarious, Camille. Absolutely hilarious."

"What is?" I asked, feeling like I was locked in some sort of trance. Maybe I was wrong. Maybe his lips hadn't thinned in displeasure but in admiration.

She laughed again, the sound more strained. "That's even funnier."

Finally Erik tore his gaze from me and I realized I hadn't done anything but stare at him. *Way to act like a sophisticated, older woman, Robins. I'm sure you're everything he's ever wanted and more, you idiot.*

"There's an empty table," I said, trying to keep my embarrassment from my tone. "Let's sit down."

"Good idea."

My heartbeat refused to slow down, slamming against my ribs with excess force. Thankfully I didn't trip—or cry or throw up. I claimed the seat facing *away* from Erik. I'd stare at him some more if I had a direct view of him, and I knew it.

I plopped my drink onto the table as Shanel eased beside me. "Is anyone looking at us now?" I asked.

"No." She sighed in disappointment.

Oh. My shoulders slumped. "Well, what are they doing?"

"They're talking to a dark-haired man wearing a black cloth over the lower half of his face. And three Morevv females," she huffed.

I heard the jealousy in Shanel's tone and experienced a wave of my own. While Morevv males were gorgeous, Morevv females were exquisite. Breathtaking. Their features were always total perfection: small, straight noses, up-tilted eyes, symmetrical cheekbones, flawless skin.

"Maybe we should go over there," she suggested.

"No!" I shouted, then felt my cheeks bloom bright. "No," I said more quietly. "Let's wait until they're alone." I wanted to talk to Erik, yes, but I wanted to do it without a group watching my every move, hearing my every word, and witnessing my every mistake.

Shanel chewed on her bottom lip. "What if they leave?"

"That's a chance I'm willing to take." Better to miss an opportunity than to humiliate myself.

A blanket of vulnerability fell over her features. "I just . . . well . . . do you think those too-gorgeous-to-live Morevvs are Silver's family? The girls, I mean?"

"Absolutely," I said, but I didn't sound convincing. Most guys I knew didn't hang out with their family at clubs. They were probably girlfriends. Or potential girlfriends. I so wanted to turn around and observe their body language with Erik. *Don't do it. Don't you dare do it.* "What are they doing now?"

"Still talking."

"Is Erik paying any attention to the women?"

"No, but they're eyeing him like he's free candy, all you can eat. It's disgusting, really. They're *old*."

Old. Great. Just what Erik liked. My jealousy intensified. I took a moment to breathe, letting my attention snag on a group of human girls just exiting the stairs. They approached the bar.

I was willing to bet they were only slightly older than me, but they looked infinitely tougher, each one radiating a palpable air that said "I'd rather kick your ass than talk to you." They were a smorgasbord of colors, from brunettes, to blondes, and even a redhead. One of the girls even had a blue trident tattooed on her cheek.

Shanel gazed from the group of guys to the group of girls I'd just noticed. "Erik paled when he saw them," she said, claiming my attention once again. "Do you think he knows them?" With barely a breath, she added, "Score! There's an empty table next to the guys. If we move, we can listen to their conversation."

I shook my head violently. "We can't switch tables. That's too obvious."

"Well, we can't just sit here, either. I've *got* to know what they're saying." She downed the rest of her drink and slammed the glass on the table. "Give me a minute to think, and—wait. I know what we can do." Reaching out, she hit my glass and "accidentally" knocked it over.

Liquid spilled toward me and I jumped to my feet with a yelp.

"Oh, damn," she proclaimed loudly. "I'm so clumsy, I knocked over your drink."

Several droplets splattered on my boots and I frowned over at Shanel. "A little warning next time would be greatly appreciated."

"Sorry. I had an idea, and I went with it." For our now-avid audience she said, "Guess we'll have to switch tables."

I almost groaned. Not so obvious, huh?

Satisfaction gleamed in Shanel's green eyes as she stood.

Someone rushed over to clean the mess so that we wouldn't have to move, but we hurriedly strode to the now empty table in front of Erik and the Morevvs. I knew they were watching us—I felt the heat of their gazes boring into me—and knew I once again sported another blush.

I hated, *hated* that I couldn't control the telltale sign of embarrassment.

We sat down and Shanel punched in an order on the wall unit for another drink. It arrived minutes later and we were left alone. Well, as alone as two girls inside of a club could get. I kept my back to the group. Call me a coward, but I still couldn't face them. Not yet.

I'd always been nervous around boys. The few I'd gone out with had been picked by my mother. Blind dates she'd set up with her coworkers' kids. Each had lasted exactly three hours. One hour for dinner and two for a movie, and each had been uncomfortable and utterly disappointing. Unlike Erik, none of them made my skin prickle with awareness and my stomach tighten in . . . I don't know what.

"Oh no!" Shanel said with a moan, cutting into my thoughts. "They're standing up."

I straightened. "Where are they going?"

Even as I spoke, I heard Erik's deep voice say, "Thank you for agreeing to move this meeting elsewhere. Too many prying eyes and ears here."

Uh-oh. *Caught,* I thought, cheeks heating again.

To my horror, Shanel waved and called, "Hi, Silver."

I sank into my chair, barely stifling the urge to cover my burning face with my hands.

"Hey," he returned, his tone wary. Confused.

A moment passed. Shanel frowned.

What had happened? Finally I gathered the courage to look. I turned in my seat and glanced over at the group. Silver had given Shanel his back, effectively ending all hope of conversation. Erik's attention was riveted on the dark-haired, half-masked man. His shoulders were stiff and his back ramrod straight.

"Come on," Half-Mask said. "You were right. The air in here is a little . . . toxic right now."

Erik nodded, his gaze sliding to the girls at the bar. Those same girls watched him, all of their eyes narrowed on him as if he were a target at gun practice. One of them, a tall, pretty Asian girl, even tipped her glass at him.

A muscle ticked in Erik's jaw.

I watched the byplay with a growing sense of dread. Did they know each other? Was she the kind of girl Erik found attractive? Probably.

In the next instant, *my* gaze connected with the beautiful Asian's. She'd stopped watching Erik and was now watching me. Me? Why? I tried not to flinch under her intense scrutiny, even though her dark, up-tilted eyes seemed to be cataloging my every flaw.

If I were brave, I would have flipped her off. But I wasn't, so I sat in my chair and did nothing. Cowardly Camille always did nothing.

My eyes widened as someone leaned toward me, getting all up in my personal space. I inched backward—until I realized it was Erik.

Shock held me immobile as his heat and pine scent surrounded me. Oh God. Oh God. Determination glinted in his dark eyes.

"I have something for you," he said huskily.

A shiver coursed the length of my spine. Not only was he close to me, he was talking to me! "O—okay," I found myself saying. Did I sound as breathless to him as I did to myself? I mean, really. This was . . . this was . . . unexpected and wonderful and everything I'd dreamed about, and I had no idea how to react.

He placed something in my hand and my fingers instantly curled around it. It was soft, a little crumpled. A napkin? Oh my God. Had he written his phone number on it? "Do you—"

He placed a finger over my lips, silencing me. "We'll talk on Monday at school." And with that, he was off.

We would talk? *More* than we already had? I watched him move away from me, so stunned I almost slid out of my chair. Seriously. Was I dreaming?

Half-Mask and the others stood in front of a guarded doorway at the back of the room, waiting, frowning. Erik said something to them, but I couldn't hear what. One of them punched in a code on a security box and they disappeared into the next room.

"Sweet baby Jesus, what did he give you?" Shanel gasped out.

"I don't know." Heart fluttering, I opened my hand. A napkin, as I'd guessed. Grinning, I unfolded the edges. The top was blank so I flipped it over. But when I saw that the other side was blank, as well, my grin faded. "I don't understand."

"Let me see." Shanel snatched it from me, looked it over, and frowned. "Is this supposed to be some sort of joke?"

The moment she spoke, realization set in. Tears burned in my eyes. A joke. Only a joke. He probably knew I had a crush on him and had done this to remind me that he was too far out of my league.

"We can't let him get away without an explanation." Scowling, she tossed the napkin back at me. "And an apology!"

I stuffed the stupid thing in my pocket, imagining whipping it out and shoving it in Erik's face. How dare he! Like I needed a reminder. I *knew*. That had never stopped me from hoping, however. Until now.

"Well? Are you going to do something?"

Stop being a coward. For once. I might be an Invisible, but I still deserved respect.

I peered at the guard posted in front of the door. He was a big, burly human beast who probably ate nails for breakfast and little children for dessert. "How can I?"

"I saw the code, and I think I know a way to get past the Hulk."

As she outlined a strategy, I paled. "I don't know," I hedged. "That seems dangerous."

"You were brave enough to come here," Shanel pointed out. "Now be brave enough to fight for what you deserve."

She made it sound so easy. "All right." I sighed. "I'll do it."

"Yes! I knew you would."

We pushed to our feet, neither knowing that we were about to set off a chain of events that could never be undone and would change our lives forever.

3

"Sir," Shanel said to the human guard. "Can I speak to you a moment?"

"Go back to your table," he growled.

"But I need to ask you something."

Scowling, he crossed his arms over his chest and braced his feet apart. "You shouldn't be in this area."

"Why not? That's what I wanted to ask you. What's back—" That's when she "tripped" and stumbled into him with all of her might, knocking them both backward and into the wall. She also poured her drink down his pants for good measure.

He howled in fury. She started crying—loudly, but not altogether realistically.

The girls from the bar rushed toward them, distracting the guard further, and I hurriedly punched in the nine-digit code Shanel had told me. The door opened and I slinked inside.

Clink.

I glanced backward and realized I'd been automatically sealed inside.

I'd done it then! I'd really done it. *Breathe, Robins, breathe.*

Trying to control my trembling, I took stock of my surroundings. I saw an empty, narrow hallway, several rooms branching from the sides. A towered ceiling with bright bulbs hanging in a line. A tiled floor. There was no sign of Erik.

Where was he?

And where was Shanel? According to the plan, she should have entered a few seconds after me. Had something happened to her? Should I go back? *Wait just a few minutes more.*

I nervously glanced around, this time looking for a place to hide.

Suddenly four hulking Ell Rollises emerged from the rooms, each holding a Lancer, I realized with nearly debilitating fear. Lancers were guns that emitted tiny, serrated stars that cut through skin and bone like butter. Another fact I'd gotten from my dad and his court cases.

Shanel must have given me the wrong code. And if they'd been ordered to hurt anyone who entered this area without authorization, I'd be hurt. There'd be no talking them out it.

This is what I got for being brave.

What should I do? What the hell should I do? I couldn't fight them; they'd destroy me in seconds.

"Innocent," I choked out. "I'm innocent."

Their beady eyes were narrowed on me. One of them even pointed his Lancer at my chest. Blood rushed from my head, leaving only panic and fear. *Run, Robins, run!* But there was nowhere for me to go.

One of them fired. A multitude of glinting, silver stars flew toward me, closer . . . closer. They seemed to be caught in slow motion, allowing me to witness every inch they gained.

With a scream, I dove to the ground.

As I fell, one of the stars made contact, sending a stream of fire through my upper arm. Another scream ripped from me as I landed in a boneless heap. Pain. Sharp, agonizing pain branched from my arm to the rest of my body.

The Outers reached me moments later, encircling me. I turned my focus to my arm, trying not to cry when I saw the blood, the ripped fabric of my top, and the gaping wound.

This could very well be the end of my life.

My entire existence didn't flash before my eyes. Instead, I saw the things I *hadn't* done. I hadn't traveled around the world. I hadn't gone to college, hadn't become an artist as I'd always wanted, hadn't had sex.

And now I'd never have the chance to do any of those things.

Shallow pants echoed in my ears, a hollow drumbeat. My skin felt chilled to the bone, yet sweat beaded over me. A violent shudder raked me. *Clink, clink.* Oh God. I squeezed my eyes tightly closed, knowing a fresh round of stars had just been loaded into the barrels of the Lancers. Any second now . . .

I love you, Mom. I love you, Dad. I'm so sorry. I never meant for this to happen.

"Stop," a cultured voice suddenly called from behind the Outers. "What's going on?"

Obeying instantly, all of the Ell Rollises froze. "We find her," one of them said. "Kill, as ordered."

"Stupid incompetents! You aren't supposed to kill until I've had a chance to question the person. Can you not think for yourselves, even for a moment? Just . . . move out of the way," the voice commanded.

A shuffling of feet. A pause.

I didn't relax. Couldn't. I'd been given a reprieve, nothing more. *You aren't supposed to kill until I've had a chance to question,* he'd said. Would he question me, *then* have them shoot me?

"Well, well, well." That disembodied voice sounded again, closer this time. "Where's your redheaded friend?"

I looked up, seeing Half-Mask. I was surprised he remembered me and who I'd been with. "Not here," I managed to squeeze past my constricted throat.

"Make sure of it," he ordered someone.

I shifted and pain once again exploded from my wound. More intense than when I'd first been shot. A whimper rose inside me, but I cut it off. If I whimpered, I'd cry and I didn't have time to cry. I had to get out of here. Had to find and warn Shanel.

Stand up! I tried, I really did. But I was simply too weak.

I watched as one of the Ell Rollises stepped over me and exited the door I'd entered. Erik and Silver approached Half-Mask, and soon all three were hovering over me, staring, taking my measure.

"Don't hurt my friend," I said. "Please. She didn't do anything wrong."

No one replied.

I focused on Erik, but his familiar face didn't give me comfort. He was frowning and I could see sparks of anger in his brown eyes. Would he let them hurt Shanel? He might. Really, what did I know about him? The boy I'd always imagined kissing wouldn't have taunted me with a blank napkin.

"Please," I found myself saying anyway.

"How did you get past the guard?" Half-Mask asked. His metallic amber eyes seemed to glow, hypnotizing me.

"I walked?" I said, the words more of a question than a statement. Right then, I wasn't sure of anything. Dizziness hit me and I moaned. With every second that passed, I became colder and yet my arm burned hotter.

I wanted to curl into a ball; I wanted to scream.

I wanted my mom.

"I do not tolerate insolence, little girl." Reaching up, Half-Mask removed the black material covering the lower part of his face.

When his appearance registered in my mind, I cringed, unable to stop the automatic reaction. His skin was puckered and colored in varying shades of red and black. He didn't have a mouth, just a gaping hole, as if someone had taken a knife and sliced him open.

"How would you like this face to be the last thing you ever see?" Those manmade lips didn't move, and it was a wonder his words were so clear, so crisp, much less understandable. "Bad little girls who sneak into places they aren't wanted earn all kinds of punishment."

"No," Erik said. He sounded as pissed as he looked. "No need for that. She's with me."

Everyone, including myself, eyed him with shock.

"You told us you told her to leave, that her kind wasn't welcome," Silver said, speaking up for the first time.

Erik's mouth edged into a tight smile; there was no amusement in the expression. "I told her to leave because I didn't want you to know I was seeing her."

"No way." Silver again. He shook his head, blue hair dancing over his forehead and temples. Then he glanced over at me, studying me with unwavering intensity. "Why would you date *her*?"

Erik shrugged, the action stiff. "Why does any guy go out with a particular girl?" His tone was dry and mocking this time.

For the second—third?—time that day, tears burned in my eyes. I let my head fall into the crock of my uninjured arm. He was letting them think he was dating me—no, sleeping with me. To save me? If so, great.

However, his attitude cut as deep as the Lancer. He spoke

like I wasn't good enough to be in the same room as him. Like I didn't deserve to breathe the same air. Like he was using me.

"I just wish the sex was better," I mumbled, pain giving me courage.

Erik blinked down at me. Silver lost his shocked expression and grinned.

"I do not like this," Half-Mask growled. "You know better than to bring a girlfriend to our business meetings, Erik."

"I'm sorry, sir." Erik didn't sound like the boy I often overheard in the halls at school. He sounded like a grown man, respectful but in no way submissive. "I should have realized she'd follow me."

"I should kill you both," the man muttered.

"I'm your best employee," Erik replied without emotion. "But more than that, her disappearance would cause unwanted media attention."

Half-Mask sighed and replaced the material over his face. "You're right. Just . . . get her out of here. Take her through the back; I don't want anyone to see her injury. If she talks . . ."

"She won't." Erik leaned down and wound his arm around my waist, careful not to touch my wound. He hoisted me up. "I'll make sure of it."

Unable to hold back my whimper this time, I swayed against him. Blood trickled down my arm, my body weakening with every second that passed. A tear finally spilled over and ran down my cheek.

"Come on," he said, leading me forward.

"Wait." Even though I was eager to escape, I dragged my iron-heavy feet. "What about Shanel?"

A muscle ticked below Erik's eye. He flicked a glance to Silver. "Will you make sure the friend gets home?"

"Safely," I added, not that anyone paid me the slightest bit of attention.

"Not the redhead who always stares at me," Silver said on a groan. "Anyone but her."

"She's the one," Erik said. "Please."

An exasperated sigh. "Yeah. Sure. Whatever. Just warn me the next time you start seeing one of the Invisibles."

"Safely," I insisted.

"Yes," Silver replied, rolling his eyes. "Safely."

Erik started walking forward again. No longer protesting, I gave him most of my weight. A strange fog was working its way through my mind, leaving a thick, black web behind.

"Erik," Half-Mask called.

We stopped. The abrupt action jolted me and I hissed. "Sorry," Erik muttered to me. Then, "Yes?" he said to Half-Mask.

"I would be very disappointed to become the focus of A.I.R. scrutiny. And you know what happens when I'm disappointed."

"You have nothing to worry about, sir. I have as much at stake as you do."

"I'm a vault," I said weakly. "Secrets are safe with me." I

closed my eyes and my head lolled against Erik's shoulder. I think an eternity passed before we stepped out of the building and into the night. Warm, clean air brushed against my bare skin, against my arm, and I wanted to scream at the sharp ache it caused.

"Which one is yours?" Erik asked.

I grit my teeth to cut off a moan. "Not mine. Shanel's." I don't know why I felt the need to point that out. Like he cared who the car belonged to. "The black sedan."

"Do you have any idea how many black sedans there are?" He growled low in his throat, exasperated, irritated, clearly pissed. "Open your eyes and at least point me in the right direction."

I did, on both counts, then closed my eyes again. How could such a small injury be so painful? How had such a promising night morphed into such a nightmare?

He led me to the car and held my hand out for fingerprint ID. My arm was so shaky I couldn't hold it up on my own.

"Now tell it to open," he commanded.

"Open," I said.

Nothing.

Erik uttered another of those menacing growls. "Is it programmed to accept your voice?"

"Yes."

"Then speak as strongly as you can, so the car recognizes you. Standing out here in the open is dangerous."

I forced a rush of air from my lungs and said, "Open!"

The car door popped open and Erik settled me into the passenger seat. "Tell the driver door to open now."

"Open," I said, even weaker than before. That door, at least, obeyed and soon Erik was settled beside me. "Accept new voice," I commanded before he could instruct me. I wasn't a complete idiot. Most days.

"Start," Erik said, and the engine instantly roared to life. He programmed in a destination and we were off.

As the car rolled along the streets and highways, heavy silence surrounded us. I was finally alone with Erik Troy, just like I'd dreamed. Yet I'd never imagined these circumstances. Me, injured and covered in blood. Him, both my tormentor and my rescuer.

"That was cruel," I said.

"What?"

"The napkin."

He didn't reply.

His silence hurt. Would it have killed him to apologize? To explain?

I kept my eyes closed and my head against the seat rest. A little while later, the whoosh of fabric cut into my thoughts, and then I felt something cool pressing against my arm.

My eyelids sprang apart and I gasped. Erik was leaning toward me, doing something to my wound. "Stop that," I commanded. "Whatever you're doing, stop."

"It needs to be done," he said flatly. "You're still bleeding."

He had taken off his shirt—and was bare from the waist up—to apply pressure to the injury. I wish I'd had the presence of mind to enjoy the sight of his tanned skin, hard muscles, and a black cat tattooed on his roped stomach. As it was, I would have rather been lying on a gurney, an IV in my vein.

"Are we going to the hospital?" I asked hopefully.

"Hell no." He scowled at me. "Do you have any idea what you've done? Do you have any idea what you could have ruined?"

His face was red with anger, his eyes bright with fury. I didn't know what I could have ruined, no, but I knew I didn't like being the target of that gaze. "I'm sorry. I didn't mean—"

"'Sorry' doesn't fix the damage you've caused. I was *this* close. This close to success, and in less than two minutes you managed to destroy all my work, making these last few months a waste."

Rather than shrink from this conflict, my normal defenses fell away and I snapped, "I'm dying, and you're yelling at me? I said I was sorry, okay? You're the one to blame here anyway. If you hadn't given me that napkin, I wouldn't have followed you."

A moment passed in silence while he ground his teeth together. Then he pierced me with a fierce stare. "One, you're not dying. You'll live. Two, once again, your 'sorry' doesn't mean shit. But it's not entirely your fault that tonight happened the way it did," he conceded. "My past finally caught up with me and things would have gone badly with or without your interference."

That mollified me, but only slightly.

"Having said that, however," he added, a steely edge to the words, "I'll tell you point three. Even if I'd given you a bag of dog shit, you should have stayed at your table. You almost blew my cover with—" He stopped himself. Frowned. "Never mind."

I blinked in surprise. "Your cover? What, you're undercover? You're a cop?"

He tangled a hand through his hair, muttering, "You wish."

"You're what, then?"

"Just drop it, Camille."

It was the first time he'd said my name. I shivered at the sound of it on his lips. "Are you A.I.R.?" It was the only other agency I could think of, and since they specialized in Outers and the Morevv had been there . . .

Erik snorted. "I'm A.I.R.'s worst nightmare, sweetheart—and now I'm yours."

4

I took a moment to digest his words.

"Ni—nightmare?" I sputtered. There was an unholy gleam in Erik's eyes, darkening the brown irises to a frightening, ominous black. He didn't look like an innocent teenager just then. He didn't look like the boy I'd crushed on for months. No, he looked mean and hard and capable of any evil deed.

A shiver moved through me, and this one wasn't pleasant like before.

"I—I don't understand," I managed to say.

"You don't need to understand," he said darkly. "All you need to know is that I've done bad things, and I'll continue to do bad things to meet my goal."

Tendrils of surprise blended with my fright. Was he threatening me? A cold chill swept through me. "I don't understand," I repeated stupidly. Surely I was mishearing, I thought, as the car hit a bump, jolting me up. I gripped my arm, trying to protect it from the stinging aftereffects.

"Like I said, I wouldn't worry about understanding. I'd worry about staying alive." He turned away from me, then, and faced the front window.

"You're just trying to scare me."

"There were A.I.R. agents in there, Camille. Remember the group of tough-looking girls?" He didn't wait for my answer. "They're after me."

"After you for what?"

"They're determined to catch me," he continued as if I hadn't spoken, "and they saw me give you that napkin. They had to wonder what was on it. A code? Information? Unless every single one of them is blind, they saw you follow me afterward. They probably think we planned the meeting and now assume you're involved with me. A.I.R. is going to be after you, as well."

A.I.R. agents. The media was fond of calling them the most feared people on the planet, saying they killed predatory aliens without thought. Without concern. Without remorse. And without a trial.

I pictured the girls, the hard gleams in their watchful eyes, the way they'd stood out, unconcerned with everything around them. The way I'd been singled out by the gorgeous Asian. Yeah, I could easily imagine her as a killer.

Don't worry. You didn't do anything wrong. "I'm innocent,"

I told Erik, my voice trembling. "And neither one of us is an alien. A.I.R. won't care what we did."

"They don't just hunt aliens. They hunt humans who help aliens commit crimes."

"But I didn't help anyone commit a crime, alien or not."

Erik just flicked me another of those hard glances.

I blinked in shock. "*You* helped an alien commit a crime?"

"Yes."

"And then they saw me follow you with that stupid napkin," I said weakly, having trouble catching my breath. "So they think . . . they assume . . ." Oh, sweet baby Jesus, as Shanel would say.

"Yes," he said again. "They think. They assume."

"How could you have done that to me?" I gasped out.

He shrugged. "I wanted them to go after you rather than me."

My shock doubled. "What?"

"They would have caught you, interrogated you, found the note blank and you as innocent as you appear, and then they would have let you go. Knowing me as they do, they would have figured out that I'd tricked them. But noooo. You had to follow me as if we'd planned it, making you look guilty as hell."

"You . . . you . . . bastard!" What he'd described *did* make me look guilty of something.

"I do whatever I have to do." Erik pinned me with his stare, holding me captive with its intensity. "Always."

I thrust my chin forward in determination. "Well, I'm going to go to them and explain what happened."

"Like they'll believe you now."

"They will."

"Whatever you say. I mean, you know how they operate, I'm sure."

My stomach churned with nausea. "I'm still going to talk to them. I did nothing wrong."

"You go to A.I.R. headquarters and you'll be beaten for information and locked away, just like me."

"You're lying."

"Only one way to find out, I guess."

My nausea intensified.

He sighed. "What if they didn't get your name? What if you're in the clear? Still think it's wise to turn yourself in?"

I experienced a ray of hope. "No."

"I didn't think so. Who knows? Because of this, you might even be able to wheedle a vacation out of Mommy and Daddy, hiding out just in case."

My mouth dried. My parents. I couldn't tell them what I'd done, what had happened. I just couldn't. I'd have to admit that I'd lied and they would be disappointed in me.

I couldn't stand their disappointment.

I was their only child, their "precious baby." I didn't want that to change. Really, one watery look from my mother and I'd want to cut out my heart. One "I thought I taught you better than this" from my dad and I'd sob.

"What if A.I.R. *does* know who I am?" I asked softly.

"They'll hunt you down, so be prepared. They'll interrogate you, asking you easy questions at first. Your name, your age. Then they'll get harder. What were you doing at the club? What did the napkin say? Why did you follow me? Have you ever dealt Onadyn and if so, who'd you get it from? Don't give them the answers they want and," he shrugged, "you'll suffer."

"Onadyn?" Feeling like I was falling deeper and deeper into a nightmare, I shook my head. Like vampires needed blood to survive, some aliens needed Onadyn. Without it . . . because of my dad, I'd seen pictures of an Outer who'd died from lack of Onadyn. The body had been contorted, the face so pain-filled it hurt me now even thinking of it.

Legally, humans were never supposed to touch the stuff. They used it to get high and often died from an overdose, so it was strictly regulated. Selling it was punishable with a life sentence.

"I have never, in all my life, even been around it!"

Erik ignored me, continuing, "They aren't bound by normal laws, so A.I.R. could even kill you if they wanted."

"But why?" A sense of hysteria built inside of me and I straightened. Hunted, interrogated, maybe killed. Surely he was lying. Exaggerating, at the very least. I was innocent, damn it.

"You're now linked to me, Camille, and I'm a suspected Onadyn dealer."

I wanted to block the words from my mind. I couldn't. They were too ominous. "But I did nothing wrong," I insisted. How many times would I have to say and think it? "I *can't* be linked to that."

"You knew the code that got you into the back of the Ship, something A.I.R. has to know is used for dealers."

"No. No, no, no. They can't find me guilty." I shook my head again, even though there were doubts in the back of my mind. "When I show them the napkin, they'll believe me."

"Or they'll think you destroyed the original and replaced it with a blank one. You've had time."

Damn him. I gripped my knees, nails digging into skin.

"I didn't ask you to follow me, Camille."

"No, you just singled me out," I said bitterly.

He flicked me a narrowed glance. "If there'd been another way . . . but I honestly expected you to leave the club. I expected you to be hauled in, questioned, and released."

That didn't excuse his actions. "Why would you get involved with something like this?" I asked. "Why?"

"I don't have to explain myself to you." His hands tightened into fists. "I hear the disgust in your voice. But guess what, Miss Innocent? Sometimes there are good reasons to do bad things."

"My dad is a lawyer, and I've heard him talk about some of his cases. Everyone has a 'good' reason for the bad things they do, but at the end of the day, other people get hurt because of those very things."

"Don't preach to me. I'm past the point of caring."

"After what you did to me, I'll preach to you if I feel like it." The car hit another bump and my arm throbbed all the more. Tears again burned in my eyes. I gazed down at the wound. Blood had already soaked through Erik's soft T-shirt.

God, could this night get any worse?

Erik sighed, losing all hint of his anger. "We need to patch you up."

"No. I just want to go home," I said softly. "That's where we're headed right?" Please, please, please.

Wait, I thought a split second later. If he took me home, my parents *would* find out I'd lied. There'd be no getting around it.

I could ask Erik to take me to Shanel's.

Nope. That wouldn't work, either. *She* was supposed to be staying with a friend, as well. Damn, damn, damn. What was I going to do?

A muscle ticked in Erik's jaw. "Drug dealer or not, I'm your only lifeline at the moment. I take you home now, and your wound will become infected. I doubt your parents know how to treat the damage a Lancer causes."

Not home then. My stomach tightened with relief—and dread. "So . . . if you're not taking me home, where are you taking me?"

"My place."

"No. No way." I might have begun the night wanting to spend time with him. Now, however, I couldn't wait to get away from him.

"Where else do you want to go, huh? And don't say 'hospital' again. Your parents will be notified and the doctors will ask you questions I don't want you to answer."

No matter what, I didn't want my parents notified. Whatever I had to do to keep them in the dark, I'd do.

More lying? I almost groaned. But if I had to, yeah. I'd lie some more. Worse than being disappointed in me, my parents would think *they* were at fault for my actions, wondering what they had done wrong, blaming themselves, moping. Just thinking about it made me hate myself.

I never should have left the house today.

Sometimes there are good reasons to do bad things, Erik had said. His voice whispered through my mind and I cringed. Lying was not a good thing, but I had a good reason for doing it—or so I told myself.

Could I trust Erik not to hurt me, though?

Probably, I decided a moment later. Despite everything he'd admitted to doing, he *had* saved me from the Ell Rollises. He'd lied for me—another good reason for a bad thing. He'd helped me to the car. He'd given me the shirt off his back.

"Will your parents mind?" I asked.

He flicked me another one of those are-you-kidding-me glances. "I don't live with my parents. I live alone."

"But how do you sup . . . port yourself?" I finished lamely. I could guess the answer: selling drugs.

"Not how you obviously think," he muttered.

Then how? Something worse than Onadyn? I wanted to ask, but didn't. Maybe it was the loss of blood. Maybe it was the fact that I'd nearly been killed. But whatever the reason, a wave of sadness overshadowed my panic, my fear, and probably my common sense. How could I have been so wrong about Erik?

There were several Onadyn addicts at our school—and Erik probably sold to them. Those kids constantly fought; they constantly stole. A few had been expelled for giving blow jobs in the bathroom. Not just the girls, either.

"Not everyone has had your pampered life." He radiated bitterness.

"You don't know anything about me." Too weak to argue with him anymore, I turned toward the side window and stared out. The moon cast golden light over crumbling buildings and the occasional tree. Slashes of color were scattered throughout, people trekking along the sidewalks and through the night. Scary people. Weapons glinted from them and their teeth flashed in evil smiles.

This was not a nice neighborhood. Did Erik live in the area? I tried not to shudder.

"You never told me," he said suddenly, cutting through the silence. "What did you do with the napkin?"

I didn't face him. "It's in my pocket."

"Good." He nodded. "Burn it when you get home."

"Of course," I lied. How many would I tell today? But no way would I burn that napkin. It was proof of my innocence. I hoped.

"I don't want them to use it against you," he said, as if reading my mind.

Both of my eyebrows arched into my forehead. "How could they?"

"I'm sure they'd find a way. They always do."

"You shouldn't have given it to me," I snapped. "You've ignored me at school all year, and the one day you pay me any attention, you practically tie weights around my ankles and toss me into a pool of sharks."

"I haven't always ignored you." His voice was even, flat.

"Liar."

"Yesterday you wore a silver heart-shaped necklace. You'd never worn it before. How's *that* for noticing?"

My mouth fell open in surprise. He was right. My parents had given me a locket yesterday morning "just because we love you." I hadn't worn it tonight because I'd been too afraid of losing it. And he'd noticed such a small detail?

Good or bad? I didn't know and considering who and what he was, I shouldn't be the least bit happy by that. No, I shouldn't. But I was. *Idiot.*

"Why were you at the Ship tonight?" he asked, changing the subject. "You've never been there before."

I ignored his question, too embarrassed by the answer. "You don't know that for sure. Maybe I've been there a thousand times and you just never saw me."

He shook his head. "You've never been there before. I would have known."

"I . . . well . . ." I didn't know what to say.

"If I didn't know better, I'd think you were sent by A.I.R."

Disbelieving, I twisted to look at him. He kept his eyes straight ahead. In profile, his nose was slightly longer than I'd realized, and his chin jutted out stubbornly. "Are you kidding me?"

"No. You show up on a night when big things are supposed to go down. You show up on the very night A.I.R. lets me know they're watching me. And finally, you eavesdrop and follow me."

My cheeks heated. Put that way, I did look guilty. Again. Apparently I'd done nothing right at the club. "And just how do you know better?" I couldn't help but ask.

There was a pause, a relaxing of his shoulders. "You don't strike me as their usual type, that's all."

"Which is?"

"Strong. Bloodthirsty. Brave."

Okay, his words really cut. Yes, I was a coward. Yes, I tended to duck rather than storm into the midst of a fight. I hated that about myself. More than that, I hated that *he* viewed me the same way.

"You're right. I'm not A.I.R." I pushed out a sigh. "Shanel and I—" God, was I really going to tell him? Was I really going to admit how stupid I was? *Why not,* I thought then. His opinion didn't matter to me anymore. Not even a little. Really. "We came to the club to see you and Silver. We just wanted the two of you to finally notice us, that's all."

Erik didn't reply—he was good at that—and my stomach tightened. What was he thinking?

I watched as the fine lines around his mouth deepened. There was a dusting of a beard on his jaw. Several boys at school had shadow beards, but now, on Erik, it made him seem infinitely older. "How old are you?" I asked.

"Too old for you," he muttered.

Ouch. "And how old is that?"

Another pause. Then, "Twenty," he admitted reluctantly.

Not so much older than me, really, but I didn't point that out. That would reek of desperation, and he already thought poorly of me—not that I cared, I reminded myself. Besides, I thought poorly of him, too!

"Twenty is a little old to still be in school," I remarked. "Did you flunk a few grades?"

He snorted. "Hardly."

"Then why—" The words ground to a halt. "Never mind." Duh. He was still in school because there was no better place to sell his drugs.

The car finally eased to a stop in front of a small, dilapidated house. The windows were sealed shut and the gray rocks were chipped and unpainted. The lawn was dry and yellowed, brittle looking.

"Welcome to my home," Erik said without any hint of pride. He exited the car.

"Open," I commanded the door. It was a weak command and the monitors didn't pick it up. I just, well, didn't want to get out of the car. That house might collapse at any moment. But Erik was at my side in the next instant, opening the door manually and wrapping an arm around my waist. He eased me to my feet.

Common sense demanded I not touch this boy who had disappointed me so sublimely, who had insulted me and considered himself better than me, despite his own stained past (and present). But I found my physical body didn't agree with my mind, and before I knew it I was resting my head on his bare shoulder. His skin was warm, smooth. He smelled good, like heat and moonlight.

Ugh. How stupid was I to still think of him that way? *He's bad, remember? Bad, bad, bad.*

"So what were *you* doing at the club?" I asked. "Buying Onadyn to sell to the kids at school?" There. The reminder chased away my enjoyment of being in his arms.

"Sometimes your smart mouth is not appreciated."

Me? A smart mouth?

He must have sensed my surprise, because he said, "Remember that little remark you made about me being a bad lover?"

Oh yeah. I almost grinned. Go me!

"Not funny," he said.

"It kind of was."

His lips were twitching as he ushered me to the front door. Because the neighborhood was so poor, I expected him to use an old-fashioned key to unlock the entrance. Instead, he had a more expensive ID box and placed his hand in the center.

Instantly a bright blue light surrounded his fingers and palm, scanning the prints.

"Welcome, Erik," a computerized voice said as the front door slid open.

Once we passed the threshold, the door closed automatically and the house lights came on. My knees knocked together and a wave of dizziness assaulted me. I swayed. Standing had been a mistake. Walking had been an even bigger mistake.

My eyelids felt as heavy as boulders and began to close on their own. Darkness winked in and out of my mind. I tipped forward.

Fall, I wanted to say. *I'm going to fall.* My mouth refused to obey.

Erik held tight, keeping me upright. "Just a little farther," he said, and I was surprised by the gentleness of his tone.

A second later, my toes hit the edge of something. The couch, I realized, when I pried my eyelids apart. It was big, brown, and soft, beckoning me to collapse.

Erik slowly spun me around and gave a gentle push to my shoulders. I couldn't do it with ease as he intended and ended up plopping down ungracefully. Plush cushions plumped around me.

"Stay here," he said.

As if I could have moved.

Finally comfortable, I fought against sleep—how good it would feel to simply doze off, to forget, to dream—and scanned the room in which I now found myself, curious to see how Erik lived.

Nothing about him had been as I expected, so why should

this? Despite the outside appearance, the inside was very nice. Vaulted ceiling, painted cement floor, gray brick walls, and clean, comfy furniture: couch (brown), love seat (brown), glass coffee table. There was even a holoscreen television.

Still, he must not sell a lot of Onadyn. Otherwise he would be living in a better neighborhood, have real wood floors, and permascented rugs. Right?

"I'm back," Erik said, at my side again. He was wearing a new shirt, I saw with disappointment—those muscles and smooth skin all covered up. In his hands he'd piled vials and bandages.

"Is this going to hurt?"

"Oh yeah."

I frowned and would have moved away if I'd had the energy. "Why'd you tell me that? You should have lied. Now I'm going to jump every time you reach for me."

He rolled his eyes. "Sit up."

I tried, I really did. But I hadn't had the strength to move from where I'd fallen, which meant I didn't have the strength to lean. Erik slid his hands behind my shoulders and urged me forward. Even my head was becoming too heavy to hold up and lolled forward.

"You falling asleep on me?" he asked.

"No," I said, closing my eyes. Why was I fighting sleep anyway? No reason to stay wake when a black chasm waited for me, begging me to fall into it. There, I could pretend this night had never happened.

"Sure?"

The single word cut through my thoughts and chased away the chasm, leaving only wakefulness and reality. No sleep for me, no reprieve. "Just bandage me up already," I muttered.

He barked out a laugh. "What I'm about to do will wake you up, don't worry."

A shiver stole through me upon hearing that uninhibited and carefree laugh. Still. I felt the color drain from my cheeks. Suffering and I were to become good friends, I guess, and were going to tango a little more tonight. "Thanks. I really needed to hear that."

"Not good with pain, I take it."

"Is anyone?"

As he unwound the shirt from my arm, I cringed and bit my lip to keep from crying. The material, soft though it was, scraped against the jagged, torn flesh. Erik said, "Some people *have* to be good with pain."

There was a strange inflection in his tone—sad, vulnerable. "You've been hurt a lot, huh?"

His gaze met mine for the briefest of seconds, but he ignored my statement. His lips pursed and he began to pinch and prod at the wound. *Ow, ow, ow.* I tried to pull from his grip.

"What are you doing? That's making it worse."

"I'm cataloguing the damage. Stay still."

Yeah, sure. "It'd probably be easier for me to wave my magic wand and produce the entire cast of *Alien Nights*."

"You actually watch that garbage?" he said, continuing the torture.

"No," I replied, cheeks flushing. Okay, maybe I'd caught an episode or two. In my defense, the other-worldly soap opera had an excellent plot. Carmine had tried to kill Sasha, who wanted to return to her home planet of Jen Jen Bi to finally have revenge on her estranged father, Escar, who had sold her to the earthling, Rocky, who hoped to produce a race of alien-human hybrids.

"You've got tissue damage." Erik straightened. "A vessel was sliced. The muscle is torn. If you hadn't ducked when you did . . ."

You could have lost the arm, I finished for him. I almost threw up. Felt bile rising, but managed to hold it back.

"This will help." He applied a thick paste to the center of the cut. A floral scent wafted to my nose. "You're lucky. Only one star hit you, and it just grazed the top layers, rather than slicing all the way through the bone."

"Feels like it's still embedded in there."

"That's because it is. Well, pieces of it." He spread a—ugh! I wrinkled my nose. He spread a foul-smelling cream over the paste. "What most people don't know is that the tips of the stars release at the moment of impact, lodging into whatever they first touch. Fortunately for you, the paste will numb everything and the cream will dissolve the metal and not the flesh, as well as cauterize the actual wound. You'll be as good as new in a few days."

I wanted to be as good as new *now*. "I've never heard of that kind of paste or cream before."

"Just because you haven't heard of them doesn't mean they don't exist. Feeling better?" he added with barely a breath.

I blinked in astonishment. Yes. I did. Truly, I'd never heard of such a fast-working medication, but I was grateful for it. The pain was already easing.

Well, the pain in my arm was easing, I realized a moment later. Now that I wasn't so consumed with the wound, I began to realize the rest of me was in pretty bad shape. Bruised, as if I'd been in a car wreck. My back throbbed—I must have jarred it when I ducked—and my thigh muscles were clenched tightly.

"You'll be weak from blood loss, so take it easy." Erik applied a final layer of gel. Thankfully, this one seemed to neutralize the cream's smell. Then he wrapped my upper arm in white cloth.

"Do you have any painkillers?" I asked. "The paste is working, yes, but the rest of me is aching now."

"Yes," was all he said.

"Well," I prompted. "Can I have one?"

He shook his head, and two locks of honey-colored hair fell over his forehead. "Nope. Sorry. The painkillers I have will put you to sleep, and I need you to stay awake."

Uh, hello. "Sleep good. Awake bad."

His lips inched into a small smile that he tried very hard to hide. "Your body will catch up to your arm, I promise.

Besides, I don't want to have to carry you to your room. Your dad might not understand."

My shoulders slumped. Yeah, that was true. My parents would freak if they saw a boy sneaking into my room. No matter the reason. Forget disappointment. They'd go ballistic. They wouldn't care that Erik had saved my life.

Thinking of the things he'd done for me confused me and warmed me all at once. I truly didn't understand how he could so coldly involve me, how he could be a drug dealer, and yet, in the end, treat me so sweetly.

Sometimes good people have to do bad things. God, how many times would that play through my mind? What exactly had he meant by that?

I must have closed my eyes and drifted to sleep (bad Camille) because the next thing I knew, a cold wet rag was pressed against my cheek. Erik cleaned my face with gentle strokes, wiping away the makeup I'd spent an hour applying. His doctoring hadn't hurt like he'd said it would. He'd been as tender as a person could be.

I might never understand him.

With that thought, my mind faded back to black. I was floating. No, not floating. I was snuggled in Erik's arms, being carried back to the car. His arms were strong and comforting as the warm night air enveloped me.

He sighed, and his equally warm breath caressed my cheek. "Come on, Sleeping Beauty," he said. "Let's get you home."

5

We didn't make it very far.

The ride began smoothly enough, and, as promised, my body did catch up with my arm and stopped throbbing completely. I was still weak, but at least I was no longer in such agonizing pain. I didn't fall back asleep, though. Couldn't. I hadn't come up with another place to go, so Erik was taking me home. Fear held me in a firm clasp as I imagined my parents' reaction when they saw me.

God, what was I going to tell them? I'd wondered before, but now that I was so close to actually seeing them . . .

"Can you take me to a motel?" I asked, desperation finally giving me an idea.

"Decided you don't want Mommy and Daddy to know what you've been up to?"

I didn't answer. "Would you?"

"Do you have money?"

"No."

"Neither do I. Besides, I wouldn't feel right leaving you at a motel."

He wouldn't feel right about it? I stiffened, but I didn't point out all the crappy things he *did* feel right about.

Seeing my renewed tension, he asked, "You doing okay?" His gaze brushed over me as surely as a caress.

I shivered—and the shiver pissed me off. Damn it. I had to stop reacting to him. Bad boys and their lives of crime weren't for me.

"Camille?"

"I'm fine."

He sighed. "No, you're not. I can hear the anger in your voice. Just tell your parents that you fell at your friend's house, you decided to come home, and she brought you. Simplicity always works best when you're lying."

Knowing my dad, he might try to sue my made-up friend to pay for damages.

"Whatever you do," Erik continued, "don't mention the club. And don't mention gunfights."

"I'm not a total idiot."

"Well . . ."

"Not all the time," I snapped.

He chuckled. "You're cute when you're mad."

Just a few hours ago, that comment would have sent me into a tailspin of euphoria. Now it—sent me into a tailspin of euphoria, I realized. It shouldn't have, but there it was. I couldn't hold back a grin.

The hottest boy at school thought I was cute.

You are *an idiot.* "How are you going to get home?" I asked when I found my voice, the dilemma just then occurring to me. "You can't keep Shanel's car."

"I know. Didn't plan to, since your friend could have already reported it as stolen and I'm eager to get rid of it."

Shanel was with Silver. She'd probably forgotten all about the car. Still. Better safe than sorry. I did not need the police looking for me, and I did not need one more supposed crime hanging over my head. "Let's call her and double check."

Without a word, Erik reached in his pocket and withdrew a small, black cell unit. He handed it to me. I dialed Shanel's number, but she never answered. I tried again. Still nothing. I didn't leave a message on her voicemail because I didn't want her parents overhearing.

I handed the phone back to Erik. I'd call her again in the morning, tell her that I had the car, and then meet her somewhere and give it back. Although, how I'd explain that to my parents, I didn't know.

"You never answered my question," I said to Erik. "How are you going to get home?"

"I'll walk," was his unconcerned response.

"Uh, that's going to be quite a hike."

"I know, but the exercise will do me some good."

He didn't need any more exercise. He was already stacked with muscle, his tanned skin stretched tight over hard steel. "You told me you were twenty years old," I said, peering at him through the thick shield of my lashes.

"Yeah. So?"

With the pain gone, my brain kicked into gear. "How'd you manage to get back into school? I'm pretty sure I know why, I just can't figure out how."

He shrugged, the action stiff. The line of his jaw ticked. In anger? In irritation? Both? "The more you know about me, Camille, the more danger you'll be placed in. Stop asking questions."

Danger. Just the word sent my nervous system into a frenzy. Heated blood rushed through my veins and caused all of my pulse points to flutter erratically. "Is that guy with the half-mask going to come after me?"

Erik paused long enough to make me squirm. Then he said, "No. I'll make sure he doesn't."

He sounded confident.

My eyes widened in horror. "Are you going to murder him?" That was the only way to give me a hundred-percent guarantee.

"No, I'm not going to murder him. Just shut up and trust me, all right."

That pacified me somewhat, but could I place my trust in someone who ignored the law and sold drugs? Someone who willingly peddled death to humans? Foolishly, I wanted to. Maybe because I was having a hard time reconciling the truth of what Erik was with the fantasy I'd built in my mind.

If he hadn't doctored me so well tonight, I *could* have written him off completely. Maybe.

"You can't seriously expect me to trust you, Erik." I only wished I meant the words wholeheartedly. "How do you know that man isn't going to come after me?"

"Camille." He sighed.

"Erik. I need to know."

He pinched the bridge of his nose. "Are you always this curious?"

"When it involves my life, yes."

"As you probably guessed, I'm working for him. He needs me and he knows it, so he won't want to piss me off."

I gazed down at my boots. Droplets of blood had dried on the tips. "And hurting me will piss you off?"

A pause, another sigh. "Yeah."

For some reason, that soothed me as I'd needed and I lapsed into silence. And, God help me, I liked, really liked, that Erik was willing to fight for me. *For your life, dummy. Not your affections. He probably doesn't want your death on his conscience—or his record.*

We passed the towering gate that surrounded my neighborhood. The houses that next came into view were medium-size, average really, but well-maintained. Made of polished silver rocks with tin rooftops, they were nearly identical. I'd lived here my entire life, and the familiarity was both comforting and terrifying.

"Uh, Camille," Erik said suddenly.

The hard catch in his voice was like a punch in the stomach, jarring, painful. Oh no. "What?"

"We're being followed."

"What!"

"Look behind us."

I twisted in my seat and peered out the back window. There were two black sedans lined up inches from our bumper, not even trying to remain hidden. Their windows were so dark I couldn't see inside. "Who is it?"

"Who do you think?

A.I.R.? I swallowed the hard lump that formed in my throat. "Lose them," I said, the instinct to remain removed from the situation speaking for me. *Please lose them.* I didn't want to be caught with Erik.

If he'd been telling the truth earlier, that would only incriminate me further. Plus, I didn't want A.I.R. escorting me home. I'd never be able to lie my way out of that.

"Why aren't you losing them?" I demanded when Erik didn't reprogram the car's destination.

"Here, let me just snap my fingers. I'll produce the cast of *Alien Nights,* too."

I ground my teeth together.

"They've been on our trail since we left my house," he added.

"Did they see me get into the car with you?"

"Maybe. Probably."

"Oh God." Stomach cramp. Not only had they seen me at the club with Erik, they'd seen me at his house. And I'd been willing. *Think, Robins. Think.*

Okay. Maybe trying to lose them wasn't the best plan of action. That would only make me appear guiltier. Maybe I should just get out, walk up to them, and explain what had happened. Maybe they'd let me go without needing to speak to my parents. Maybe my worries were for nothing.

According to Erik, A.I.R. fought to protect innocent humans. I was innocent. But also according to Erik, A.I.R. would beat me up first and ask questions later. Well, what's it going to be?

"I—I'm going to talk to them."

"I can't let you do that," Erik said. "No telling what you'll admit to doing."

"But—but—"

He commanded the car to stop. Tires squealed, and I strained against my seat belt.

"Erik! What—"

"Shit," he growled.

A black sedan had come out of nowhere, blocking our forward path. We couldn't advance and we couldn't reverse. They had us pinned in.

"Just let me out," I said. "They'll be reasonable about this. They just have to be."

"They won't listen to a damn thing you say." Motions clipped, Erik punched a series of buttons on the console keyboard. The lights dimmed, and a gear shift I think it was called, rose from the space between us. Panels opened in a wide circle and a steering wheel appeared. Pedals even lifted from the floorboard.

I'd seen this happen on TV, but never in real life. Fear gripped me. "What are you doing?" I managed to get out.

"Overriding the computer system and driving manually."

"You can do that?" Duh. He just had.

"Just hold on to your seat. It's gonna get bumpy." Without another word, he jammed the gear backward and the car speed into reverse. *Crrrunch.*

I yelped. Metal ground against metal as we crashed into one of the sedans, then Erik moved the gear forward, turning the wheel, turning, turning.

We hit another car.

He slammed his foot into one of the petals. My entire body flew toward the windshield as we sped away from our tails and onto a side road. Thankfully my seat belt pulled me back.

The other cars, of course, followed us. Their tires screeched, burning rubber and wafting smoke in every direction.

Fear raced through me, stronger than ever before. Stronger, even, than when I'd been surrounded by aliens, Lancers pointed at my chest. Not only was I in danger now, but innocent people were, as well. Anyone taking a nighttime stroll . . . I clutched my stomach to ward off another cramp.

"Erik. You have to stop this."

"Can't."

"Please."

"What I do is too important. I can't be locked up."

"*What* do you do?" I asked, nearing hysteria. "Helping humans kill themselves isn't important."

His lips drew together in a thin line.

"What if we're wrong and those drivers aren't with A.I.R.?" I asked sharply. I squeezed my eyes shut when we ran over a recycling bin and jumped a curb. *My God, who art in heaven.*

"They're A.I.R."

Tires squealed as our car jacked a swift left turn. *Hallowed be thy name.* Or was it "hollowed"? "How. Do. You. Know. That? For sure?"

"Call it a hunch," he said dryly.

Breathe, Camille. Just breathe. In. Out. Slowly. Slowly. Okay, I could handle this. I wasn't in the midst of a car chase. I was at the beach, a cool breeze billowing around me. Sun rays were soaking into my skin and saltwater was brushing against my toes.

Tires squealed again, ruining the fantasy. We executed a swift right turn and I was flung into the door.

Any more, and I'd throw up.

"There's got to be a better way, Erik."

"I'm open to suggestions."

If only I had one. He hit a bump and my nausea intensified. Motion sickness—maybe. Another injection of pure fear—probably.

"Close your eyes," he commanded.

"They *are* closed!"

In the next instant, I was lifted out of my seat. My head skimmed the roof. And I knew what had happened: we'd gone airborne. Erik whooped excitedly. I commanded my window to open, leaned over, and emptied out the contents of my stomach, jerking with the force of the action. My ribs ached and my back tightened even after I'd slumped back in my seat.

My cheeks heated with embarrassment. Oh. My. God. I'd just thrown up in front of Erik Troy. At least I hadn't done it on the floorboards, so we didn't have to smell it. Still. Could I be any more disgusting? No time to ponder that now. The car landed, and it landed hard. *Boing. Thud.* My throat constricted, cutting off my airway. A wave of dizziness swept through me.

Left, right, left, we turned. "You okay?" Erik asked.

I nodded, unable to speak.

"There's a water bottle in the bag at your feet. Might help you calm down."

A bag? I looked down and sure enough, there was a black vinyl bag. I bent and dug through it, finding a change of clothing, an oddly shaped pair of sunglasses, and yes, a bottle of water. Straightening, I chugged the contents, swishing my mouth out with every gulp.

"I think you're wrong about them," I said, forcing the

words out. "What can it hurt to let me talk to them? It can't make our situation any worse." I hoped.

He snarled low in his throat.

I took that as a no. Dear Lord. Innocent schoolgirl one day, shot at, chased criminal the next. *Don't think like that. You're not a criminal. Yes, things look bad, but after you explain the situation everything will be fine.* "Please, Erik."

"Have you listened to nothing I've said? They'll shot first and ask questions later."

Light-headed, I buried my face between my knees. We hit a curb and bounced again. "Maybe I prefer to be shot at than smashed around."

"It's going to be okay, Camille."

I caught traces of uncertainty and guilt in his voice. "I know," I offered, trying to comfort *him.* Silly girl.

"I think we're going to have to ditch the car. Think you've got the strength to run?"

"Sure," I replied, knowing I wouldn't have to prove it. When he stopped, I was going to turn myself in.

"Good, 'cause running is the best chance we've got."

A humorless laugh escaped me. "I've never made less than a B in school, I hardly ever break the rules, and I avoid conflict like it's toxic waste. I made one mistake, just one, and this is what I get. I'll never try to impress a boy again."

"It's gonna be okay," he repeated more gently this time.

"Forget A.I.R. Shanel might never forgive me for losing her car."

"You won't have lost it. You'll simply have to let it be im-pounded."

Like that was any better. Maybe I'd have to tell my parents the truth after all. If I lied and got caught later, that would only increase my list of ever-growing sins. "That will draw Shanel into this mess. Which will eventually lead to meeee—" The word sputtered in my throat as we ground to an abrupt halt.

I sat up. Immediately I saw that a large brick wall blocked our frontward path. All three black sedans surrounded us in seconds, left, right, and behind.

Once again, we were pinned in.

"I guess you were right," Erik muttered. He didn't sound upset. "I should have found a better way."

Only darkness and brick greeted us. And disaster. Yes, di-saster. The cars flashed high beams of light directly on us, il-luminating everything they touched.

I faced Erik. He might have sounded unconcerned, but his expression was tight, furious, and his brown eyes were sparkling. I could see the glint of pyre-guns pointing at us, and suddenly wasn't so sure I wanted to turn myself in. "What should we do?"

His hands tightened on the wheel. "Like before, I'm open to suggestions."

"Just—" What?

"Do you have a weapon?" he asked me.

Oh God. Weapon equaled blood and blood equaled pain.

"No. And I don't want one. A gunfight is not the way to end this."

Erik scrubbed a hand down his face. "You're right. If I was alone, I'd fight. With you here . . ."

With me here, he ran the risk of what? Hurting me? Oh God, oh God, oh God.

"Get out of the car," a female voice suddenly echoed around us. "Both of you. Hands up and out."

Erik didn't move. Neither did I. My heart galloped in my chest, trying to beat its way through my ribs inch by inch. "Erik," I said. I didn't know what else to say. I was so scared.

"Don't look at me," he said.

"Why?" I faced forward, but from the corner of my eye I watched as he moved his arms behind his back and withdrew a pyre-gun from the waist of his pants. Every ounce of moisture in my mouth dried, leaving only the taste of cotton and bile.

"I thought you didn't want to fight," I asked, the panicked words nearly inaudible.

"I don't want to die, either."

Die. I swallowed. If things ended badly, I could die a virgin; I *would* die a loser who'd supposedly dabbled in Onadyn. "Erik," I said. "This is crazy. This is wrong on so many levels."

He stared down at the weapon, as if he wasn't quite sure what he wanted to do with it. Yellow beams of fire were projected from pyre-guns, scorching everything in their path. Human, nonhuman. Didn't matter. Another little tidbit I'd picked up from my dad and television.

"Erik," I repeated, his name a hoarse entreaty.

"Hell," he grumped.

"Get out of the car!" the female voice said again. "Now! I'm sick of waiting."

I gulped. "I'm going to get out now."

"I'm going to create a distraction," Erik said. "You're going to run."

I gaped at him. I could see the long length of his lashes casting shadows over his cheek. Bleak shadows, frightening shadows.

"Understand?"

"No. I told you. Running now is stupid. Just give yourself up."

A muscle ticked under his left eye. "Everything will turn out okay if you'll run and stay hidden until I can somehow clear your name."

"But—"

"No buts. You're innocent, and I dragged you into it. You shouldn't have to deal with this." He paused, then finally studied me. He growled low in his throat. "Promise me, Camille. Promise me you'll run and not look back."

"That just makes me look all the more guilty."

Our pursuers lost any hint of patience and flashed their lights. "Get out of the fucking car. I'm close to blowing it to pieces. Feel me?"

"They'll hurt you, Camille," Erik said, still not moving from the vehicle. The dark brown of his eyes pierced me deeply. "They'll beat you and they'll torture you for answers you don't have. Don't try and be a hero tonight."

Ha. I'd never tried to be a hero in my life. But more than making me look guilty, leaving him meant letting him endure questions about *me,* I suddenly realized. *He* might be beaten. *He* might be tortured.

"I'll stay," I said, determined. "Maybe we can convince them that you—"

"You won't explain because you're not staying." Erik reached behind him a second time, angling his arm up and somehow anchoring the gun at the back of his neck, making sure the high back of the seat hid his actions from the agents. "Don't worry about me. I'll be fine. I always am."

He was lying, and we both knew it.

He didn't give me a chance to respond, though. "It's been nice knowing you, Camille. Now get ready to run," he mumbled, and then he opened the car door.

6

I can do this, I mentally chanted. *I can do this. I'm smart—sometimes,* I added. *I'll* make *them listen to me.* I just wished my nervous system would calm down. Blood raced through me, hotter than fire, burning, burning. A loud ringing echoed inside my ears.

Erik emerged from the car, hands at his sides. He pasted a cocky, come-and-get-me grin on his face. I stayed where I was, scared, trying to force the right words into my brain and yeah, praying this was a bad dream and I'd awaken any second.

"Hands up," the voice said, and he slowly obeyed. "Camille Robins, get out on your side of the car."

Hearing my name, I gasped in surprise. They *had* already figured out who I was. There would have been no reprieve for me, no matter how far I'd run or where I'd hidden.

Voice shaky, I commanded the car door to open. The moment I stood outside, I had to blink against the brightness of the halogens. My eyes even teared. "We're innocent," I said. My legs were so weak I could barely hold myself up and had to latch onto the car.

"Hands up," the voice shouted.

I let go and almost fell again. I had to lean my shoulder against the car for support.

"She's injured," Erik said loudly, then whispered to me, "Almost time to run."

"I'm staying," I whispered back.

"We'll see."

"I want to explain about tonight," I called, trying to give details that helped both of us. I truly didn't want him hurt, either. "I'd never really spoken to Erik until tonight, so we couldn't have planned anything together. We—"

Erik cursed, and I realized our captors were racing toward us. Erik whipped the pyre-gun from its perch on his neck and started firing. Yellow-orange beams cut through the golden lights, through darkness, illuminating the shapes of three women. Each of them dove for cover and immediately shot back, their fire slamming into our car. Some were aimed directly at *me*.

I screamed and ducked. "I'm unarmed!"

Another blast hit just behind where I'd been standing.

Erik returned a steady stream of fire and worked his way behind the open driver-side door, using it as a shield.

"Run," he shouted to me.

On instinct, I managed three crawl steps. Then I froze. *What are you doing? You can't leave!*

"Run, you idiot," Erik growled.

"No."

Just then, a stream of yellow fire whizzed past my ear. It didn't touch me, but it was so hot my skin instantly blistered. My stomach twisted painfully and I scrambled behind the passenger door.

"She isn't fucking armed," Erik shouted to the women.

"Drop your weapon," someone shouted back. A girl, different from the one who had first spoken.

"Like hell," he told her. He fired another shot and I heard the girl curse under her breath.

Yeah, I knew the feeling. I wanted to curse and scream and curse some more. "You have to believe me. We're innocent. Everything that happened tonight was a big misunderstanding."

"The shot that grazed you was a warning, Camille," one of the girl's said, fury dripping from her voice. "Next time I'm aiming for your heart. You want to live, you'll walk toward me, hands up. We'll go someplace quiet and talk."

I made to straighten, and a beam hit just above my shoulder. Screaming, I ducked. *Were* they trying to kill me? "I thought—I thought—"

"They want you injured," Erik explained. "They'll say anything to get their hands on you."

"But I *am* injured!" And I no longer wanted to give myself over to these girls. I think, perhaps, I was safer with Erik.

"No, you're trapped," a third female voice said, this one a purring rumble. "Much as I'd like to scratch your eyes out, Erik, we have orders to bring you in unharmed. If possible. But I don't care who the hell you are. It's open season on you *and* your little friend if you keep firing."

Her words confused me. Who was he to them?

A second later, bright amber light exploded, consuming the night's darkness, brighter than the halogens, glowing and shining over me and Erik. No shadows remained.

We were spotlighted.

"Let Camille go, and I'll give myself up," Erik shouted. "My aim hasn't been off, either, ladies. If I wanted you dead, you'd be dead."

Someone laughed. Someone else snorted. *I* reeled. He would give himself up for me?

"Whatever you say, Erik," the one with the scratchy, purring voice said.

"We'll let her go, no problem," another said.

I think she was in charge since she was the first to have spoken to us and had an authoritative ring to her voice that the others didn't have. But even I knew she was lying—though I might have wished otherwise. No one shot at you only to let you go without incident.

"We really are innocent," I said, trying again to make them understand as I squinted against the brightness of those stupid lights. Well, *I* really was innocent, at least. I couldn't see the girls, not even a hint of them. I could see only orange and gold spots and the darkness that surrounded them, a darkness I wanted to be a part of. My eyes once again watered and I had to look down at my boots. "The napkin you saw him give me is blank. And I followed him because I was mad at him. I wanted to ask him why he gave it to me. That's all."

"Sounds like an interesting story and one I'd like to hear in more detail."

I wish I could see them, judge their expressions.

"Surely you can agree to come in and talk to us." This new voice was placating, soothing.

Good cop to the other two bad cops, perhaps. "I tried. You shot at me."

"Give me another chance. I'll play nice."

"Don't listen to them, Camille," Erik barked.

I leaned my forehead against the coolness of the car door. My arm hung limply at my side, useless. My knees knocked together. I couldn't have moved if my life depended on it.

Maybe it did.

"You run and hide until everything's settled," he said, "just like I told you."

"For the last time, I said no!"

"What are you two arguing about over there?" the leader asked.

A hand suddenly cupped my shoulder and I gasped. I whipped my attention to the side, breath congealing in my throat. When I saw who was crouched behind me, I almost melted into a puddle of relief. Erik.

His expression was hard, guarded. "You should have run." He didn't look at me as he spoke, but kept his attention straight ahead.

"I couldn't. You would be in way more trouble."

His hand settled on my lower back. "You keep surprising me, Camille Robins."

I kept surprising myself.

"I'm getting tired of waiting," the purring one called. "I haven't met my kill ratio this week, and you're seriously pressing your luck."

"Blow up the car then," Erik taunted. "Our time is up anyway."

I paled. Had he just told them to blow up our car?

"Don't tempt me. A lot of people want you dead, Erik. I just want to talk to you."

If I'd had the strength, I would have slapped my hand against Erik's mouth so that he couldn't respond. As it was, he didn't incite her further. "Give me a moment to think," he called.

"You don't have any options but death or surrender."

"Let me think, damn it!"

Pause.

"One minute," came the response. "And the countdown begins now. If you haven't made a decision by then, I'll make it for you. I've already given you more leeway than I've ever given any other. The fact that we were once friends is beginning to mean less and less."

"So why'd you do it?" he said quietly. "Why'd you really stay with me?"

A moment passed before I realized he was talking to me. "We have one minute and you want to talk about this *now*?"

"Yes. So hurry."

"They already knew my name," I replied, trying to absorb his strength. His hair hung low, covering his eyebrows. There were frown lines around his mouth. And yet, he'd never looked sweeter.

"You didn't know that until a minute ago. Why?" he persisted.

He wanted the truth. Fine. I had nothing to lose at this point. "I couldn't just leave you here to die."

"Even though I ignore you at school?"

"Even though."

"Even though you think I'm a drug dealer?"

I caught the phrasing and blinked. He'd said "you think." Not "I am." In that moment, hope that he was just a regular guy who'd been misunderstood bloomed and spread. "Yeah."

His expression had become vulnerable. Soft. As hopeful as I felt.

"Even though."

"Stupid," he said, but there was a lightness to his tone that hadn't been there before. "Brave." And then he turned toward me and placed a soft kiss on my lips, shocking me.

The kiss didn't last long, but it shook me to the core.

Danger was all around us and there was a mental tick-tock in my mind, but I didn't care. Erik Troy had just given me a kiss. Not with tongue, like I'd dreamed of so many nights, but with caring—as if we were about to die and he wanted to savor his last few minutes on Earth.

Even though the kiss had stopped, he didn't immediately pull away. I breathed in his scent, as warm and crisp as the night, basking in this stolen moment. So badly I wanted his arms to wrap around me, to hold me close.

But they didn't, and I understood why. He couldn't remove his gun from the girls' sights. A sobering thought. And yet, this still managed to be the happiest moment of my life.

Maybe because, for the first time in my life, I realized I wasn't promised a tomorrow. Maybe because I'd crushed on him for so many months. Either way, I took comfort from the action. My determination to make it through this ordeal (alive) intensified.

"I'm not worth staying for," he said. "Ever."

A few minutes ago, I might have agreed with him. With that "even though you think I'm a drug dealer" comment, I wasn't so sure anymore. "Let me be the judge of that," I replied.

He studied me for a moment. "I don't know what to make of you. You're—" Suddenly he squeezed off a shot in the girls' direction. "Do *not* come any closer, Phoenix."

"Damn it, Erik!"

"You promised me a minute, and I've got a few seconds left."

Phoenix. Hearing him say a name reminded me of the familiarity he had with these girls. "You know them?"

"Yeah. Unfortunately."

"I'm getting tired of this, Erik," Phoenix, the leader, growled. "You can't hold us off all night."

"Listen, we both know I have information you want. You're not going to rush in and fight me."

"You used to be one of us," a new voice proclaimed.

Erik stiffened. A look of absolute defenselessness passed over his expression. "Cara?"

"Yeah," Cara said, her voice hard, stiff. "I'm here, too. You almost killed me with your stuntman driving."

Why had he stiffened? Why the defenselessness? And he'd once been an A.I.R. agent? He did seem to know a lot about them. And I'd never seen anyone use a weapon quite so expertly.

"You may not want to fight us," Cara said, "but I'd love to smash your face in."

Ex-girlfriend, I decided with a twinge of jealousy. "How long have you two been broken up?" I asked before I could stop myself.

Erik shrugged, pulling his attention back to me. "How'd you know we dated?"

I tapped a fingertip to my temple. "Smart."

"A few months," he said with a small grin.

"What'd you do to make her so mad?"

His lips pursed, destroying all hint of that grin. "Not a good time to discuss that."

"Just like you know we won't kill you," Cara added as if there had never been a lag in their conversation, "we know you won't kill us."

"You don't know anything about me," he growled darkly. "Not anymore. Maybe not ever."

Pause.

"I'm approaching, and if you singe a single hair on my head I'll kill you the way I've wanted for months," Cara said.

"Sure you want to risk it, babe?" he said to her. "I've wanted to hurt you, too. I've dreamed of it, in fact."

Babe? Babe! Did he still have feelings for her? None of my business, it didn't matter, *shouldn't* matter, but . . . obviously, he did still care and obviously I did, too. He'd kissed me, after all.

Plop.

My brow furrowed. What had made that sound?

"I dropped my gun," Cara said, answering my unspoken question. "I'm weaponless."

Erik snorted and peeked over the car window. "But you're never defenseless."

I, too, peeked through the window and watched as a beautiful Asian girl stepped into the light. She had smooth, caramel-colored skin, almond-shaped brown eyes, and rich, dark hair pulled back in a ponytail. She was medium-size and lithe, her smooth curves encased in tight, black syn-leather.

My head tilted to the side and I frowned. She'd been at the Ship. She'd been in that group of girls who had watched Erik so intently. *She* hadn't watched Erik the whole time, though. She'd mostly watched me.

Had she suspected me of working with him, even then? Dear God. Maybe the night had been doomed to fail no matter what I'd done. The girls as they'd walked up to the bar replayed through my mind . . . one of them had a blue trident tattooed on her face, one had pale hair and pretty features. One had brown hair and a sharp gaze. I couldn't recall the others, though. I only knew that there *had* been others.

Were they all here? Probably. My stomach twisted with the thought. That meant we couldn't see them all; some had to be hiding. Maybe even sneaking in behind us.

"There's more, Erik. There's more!"

He understood what I was saying. "I know. Three have already worked their way in front of the car. The building is keeping them from having a clear shot, though, so don't worry."

Don't worry? Don't worry!

If Erik knew these girls so well, why hadn't he left the Ship the moment he'd spied them? I know he'd seen them. He'd stiffened and moved his meeting with Half-Mask to another room.

To save innocents in case a gunfight broke out?

"Damn it, Cara," he suddenly snarled.

Cara continued to walk toward us, maintaining a slow and steady pace. Strands of her dark hair wisped around her lovely face. "That isn't what you used to say to me. You used to be happy to see me."

No wonder Erik hadn't ever asked me out; he used to date perfection.

"That was a long time ago," Erik told her.

"And a lot of things have changed since then. Including your appearance. Thought we wouldn't recognize you with a different hair color? Thought we wouldn't find out you'd had eye surgery, replacing your own peeps with someone else's? You looked better with green eyes, I must say."

"Stop!" he shouted, gruff. "I don't want you any closer."

If she reached us . . . Lord, I didn't know. What would she do? Nothing good, that much was obvious. There was fury in her pretty brown eyes. And what would Erik do? He obviously didn't want to hurt her or he would have fired by now.

For the first time since this night of terror had begun, Erik appeared deeply and unequivocally scared—and that frightened me all the more.

I mean, if *he* was scared, something terrible was about to go down. Every warning he'd given me about A.I.R. flashed through my mind. Pain. Torture. Death. So far, he'd been right about everything else.

If he wouldn't protect us, I had to.

Gulping, I searched the area for some sort of weapon. I saw dirt, gravel, brittle blades of grass. A few rocks. Then I saw the handle of a gun sticking out of the waist of Erik's pants. I'd never handled a gun before. They weren't even allowed in my house because my dad abhorred violence of every kind.

Before I could talk myself out of it, I grabbed the weapon and aimed it at Cara. I didn't fire, just shouted, "I have a gun and I'm not afraid to use it." *That's so lame, Robins!*

Erik jerked in surprise, reached out for me, then thought better of it and stilled. Cara, too, froze in place.

"He might not shoot you," I said, "but I will." Maybe. Oh hell. *What are you doing?*

"Innocent, huh?" A look of disgust washed over Cara's delicate features. "Get control of your girlfriend, Erik," she snapped, stepping forward again.

My hand trembled. "I'll shoot. I will. I just want you to stop and listen to what I have to say. Don't threaten us anymore. All right?"

"Hand me the gun," Erik said, trying to sound calm but not doing a very good job of it. "Just hand it over and everything will be fine."

"No." Tears stung the corners of my eyes. "They aren't listening to us! And you were right. They shoot first and ask questions later."

"Camille," he said.

"No!"

Cara took another step, so close I could see the golden highlights in her hair. I could see the matching flecks of gold in her eyes.

"Camille," Erik repeated. "You don't want to do this."

No, I didn't.

He reached out slowly and wrapped his fingers around mine. His touch was gentle; I could feel the callus on his palm, a little abrading. "They'll never believe you're innocent if you start shooting."

"But—"

"You don't know the things they're capable of. Don't become their enemy."

"I think I might already be their enemy," I whispered, desperate.

"I won't let anything happen to you. Okay? Trust me. I'll take care of you. I've taken care of you up to this point, haven't I?"

"Well . . ."

"From now on then."

Cara reached the door, her booted feet touching mine. The gun pressed into her chest. "You didn't used to make promises you couldn't keep."

"Shut the hell up, Cara. She *is* innocent. I'll come in and explain." Erik paused, his eyes never leaving me. "Camille. Give me the gun."

A tear escaped and slipped down my cheek. I allowed Erik to take the gun from me. My shoulders sagged in relief.

I hadn't really wanted to shoot anyone anyway and I'd never been good at confrontation.

In the next flash of time, Cara gave her arms a single shake and two blades fell into her waiting hands. Before I could blink, she had the sharp tips at Erik's throat.

I gasped in shock, in horror. "You said you were unarmed."

"I lied." She didn't face me. I guess she didn't consider me enough of a threat. "He's subdued," she called. "Aren't you, baby?"

Erik remained silent. Our gazes met, and he gave a single shake of his head meant to assure me that everything really would be okay.

The other girls rushed forward and I saw that I'd been right. There wasn't just three or four of them. There were six of them. Someone, the one with the blue trident tattoo, grabbed me and shoved me to the ground, face-first. Dirt filled my mouth and I tried to spit it out.

"Don't hurt her," Erik commanded. "I told you. She's innocent in all of this. I gave her the napkin to distract you."

"She's as innocent as you, I'm sure," Cara scoffed.

My arms were jerked behind my back and I screamed so loud and long the sound echoed through the night. The action had caused the numbness in my wound to wear off abruptly and I felt every new throb of pain.

Erik grabbed Cara's wrists and gave a sharp twist. She tumbled to her knees with a yelp, her blades falling to the ground.

He dove for me in an effort to free me, but someone—a human cat?—met him halfway and they tumbled together on the gravel.

"Let her go," he snarled. "You're hurting her."

Erik and the girl, who had multicolored hair and pointy ears, struggled and rolled on the ground. The girl hissed and lashed out with her nails. Erik didn't punch her, as I would have liked him to do, but he dodged her blows and struggled to pin her.

"Careful with him, Kitten," Phoenix growled. "I want him alive."

"Yeah, well," the purring one said. "You want me alive, too? He's fighting dirtier than when we last rumbled with him." She grunted as Erik flipped her over his shoulder.

She held onto him, pulling him back down. Her orange, red, and black hair formed a curtain around them. Moving with the grace and fluidity of a cat, she arched her back and slid herself up Erik's body. She was a Teran, I realized.

Captured as I was, I didn't know what to do, how I could help. So I said, "Erik, it's okay. I'm okay."

Cara had reclaimed her knives and leapt at the dueling pair. Distracted, Erik didn't see her and soon Cara's blades were once again compressed against his throat. Several droplets of blood cascaded down his neck.

And yet, still he fought to get to me.

"I'm okay," I repeated, fighting past the pain. "I'm okay."

This time, he stopped moving. Panting, he moved his

gaze over me to judge the truth of my words. I had a feeling that he would have started struggling again if I'd so much as frowned.

With Cara pressing the knife into his throat, the one called Kitten wound laserbands around his wrists. Laserbands were wound around my wrists, as well, their light bonding to my skin. If I tried to take them off, I'd take hunks of skin and bone with them.

"Now that that's taken care of," Phoenix said. She stood in front of us and dusted off her hands. She was the girl with the blonde hair and brown eyes. Pretty, almost fragile-looking—a startling contrast to the aura of death that blanketed her expression. "Let's get these two to A.I.R. lockup. I've got questions. They've got answers."

7

Erik and I were shoved into separate cars. At that point, everything became surreal to me. One minute I'd been at a club with my best friend, scoping out my crush, the next I'm injured and the prisoner of a group of people who'd so far proven themselves to be ruthless.

What could I do? I'd mentioned the napkin, I'd tried to explain what had happened, but so far no one had cared to listen to me. Not even when I'd held that gun.

I was beginning to suspect, deep in my bones, that they might never believe me, no matter what I said. In their minds, I was guilty and that's all there was to it.

Trying not to panic, I slumped in my seat. No one had bothered to shut the passenger door, so I heard the girls as they laughed proudly about their capture and taunted Erik.

"Thought you'd escape us, did you?" one of them said.

"You should have known we'd catch up to you sooner or later," another proclaimed. "We always do."

"You never were very bright," still another chortled.

He didn't respond, but even from this distance I could see the hurt in his dark eyes—eyes that had once been green, apparently. I tried to picture him with green eyes but couldn't. How could they be so cruel to him?

Our doors were shut, blocking him out completely. Each of the girls claimed a car. A blonde I didn't recognize turned out to be my driver, and Cara settled in beside her.

She didn't speak to me, but cast me narrowed glances every few minutes. A glass partition separated us, so I couldn't talk to her. That was okay. At the moment, I despised her. And, I hated to admit, I was scared of her. She'd lied, she'd attacked. She'd *won*.

Worse, Erik's ex-girlfriend might very well hold my future in her hands.

———

Thirty minutes and a bumpy ride later, we were parked in an underground garage that led to a stone-and-glass fortress. Towering, oppressive, eerie, the building practically screamed "keep out or die." People strolled in and out, and all of them wore black syn-leather and had pyre-guns strapped to their waists.

I didn't see Erik as the blonde jerked me from the car. She

flanked one side, Cara flanked the other, and they escorted me inside. I tried not to cringe at the pain in my arm. I tried not to cry.

What were they going to do to me?

"This is all a big misunderstanding," I tried explaining yet again.

"Yeah. I believe you," Cara said dryly. " 'Cause I'm an idiot."

"If you'd just listen—"

She pressed my shoulder, hard, and I gasped. Then she pressed harder and my knees gave out. Neither girl did anything to stop my ensuing fall. I yelped, hitting the ground face-first. Air shot from my lungs in one mighty heave.

I lay there for a moment, stunned. *They won't hurt me,* I'd told Erik more times than I could recall. How foolish I'd been. I uttered a humorless laugh as I tried to tamp down another surge of fear. "It's illegal to treat me this way. I haven't been found guilty of a crime."

"We don't need to find you guilty," Cara said. "We just need to suspect."

"Call my father," I found myself saying. He would protect me. Yes, he'd find out everything I'd done, how I'd lied, but I no longer cared. I suddenly wanted away from these girls, no matter what.

"We'll call him. Later."

"I know my rights." My dad had made sure of it. "I'm a minor. You have to call him if I request it."

"If we were dealing with a human crime, sure. With Onadyn, all bets are off. Besides that, you are so not a minor. You're eighteen. Legally an adult."

"He's my attorney." I tried to push myself up, but Cara jammed her foot on my back, slamming me back down. I winced.

"No getting up yet," she said. "I like you where you are."

"This is harassment. This is assault," I huffed, anger pushing past my fear. "Let. Me. Up."

"Think you're tough enough to make me?" Cara chuckled and there was a menacing edge to the sound. "If so, you'll soon learn better. I'll make sure of it."

She removed her foot and the blonde jerked me to a standing position. At the wide double doors, she secured me against a wall so that I couldn't run as she and Cara endured a palm and retinal scan. The entrance opened and I was tugged inside.

People—agents, I'm sure—were everywhere. Behind desks, walking the plain, silver hallways. Few spared me a glance. There were holoscreens, computers, and other equipment I didn't recognize.

"This isn't—" I pressed my lips together. *Whatever you say can be used against you in a court of law.* I felt the heat drain from my skin as my dad's voice echoed in my mind.

"Say hello to your new home," Cara told me. "Your weight, height, and body heat have already been logged into the system. You step foot in this lobby or any of the surrounding rooms without permission and you'll be dead."

A tremor worked through me.

After several twists and turns, we finally reached a steel door. We lost the blonde somewhere along the way. Cara had to pause for another scan, this one a full body. Red lights pulsed over her seconds before the door opened.

This new hallway boasted several other doors that led straight into prison cells. The knowledge nearly undid me. I was shoved inside the last room on the right. The air inside was sterile-smelling. There was a chair in the center, but that was it.

Another tremor catapulted the length of my spine. My new home, she'd said. For how long?

"Put your face against the wall," Cara commanded me.

For a split second, I thought about disobeying. In the end, I didn't. *Coward.*

The moment my cheeks pressed against the cool metal, she was behind me, removing my laserbands. I felt a tug on my wrists and then, finally, the heat of the bands was gone.

"What's your full name?" she asked, her voice cold, emotionless.

"Camille Diane Robins."

"How old are you, Camille Diane Robins?"

They'll ask you easy questions at first, Erik had warned me. *Then they'll get harder.* I had trouble catching my breath, but managed to gasp out, "Eighteen. You already know that."

She stared over at me for a long while, studying me, and it looked like a war raged in her mind. Finally she nodded, as if she'd made a decision. "I'll be back for you in a little bit. For now, you can sit here and think about all the ways I'm going to hurt you if you lie to me."

Oh, I'd imagine, all right. Needles shoved under my nail-beds. Hammers pounded into my knees. All of my hair shaved off. But I couldn't let that affect me. Today I'd endured the sting of a Lancer. I'd lived through a car chase and a gunfight. I hadn't cracked to a million pieces when this girl pushed me down. *Time to stop being a coward.*

"Where's Erik?" I asked, turning to face her eye-to-eye. A brave move, one I wouldn't have attempted any other day. But I wanted to talk to him. He'd told me what to expect. Now I wanted him to tell me what to do, and how to get out of here. *How is* that *any better?*

She raised one brown brow. "What do you care? What's he to you?"

"A hero, I guess. He fought to protect me while *you* were shooting at me."

Anger washed over her lovely face, vibrating palpably. "You think that makes you special? Well, it doesn't. He once saved my life, too."

I blinked at her in surprise. "How can you treat him this way then?"

She didn't answer. In fact, she spun on her heel and strode out of the room, leaving me alone. Alone to wonder.

Where had they taken Erik? What were they doing to him?

Had my parents been notified as I'd requested?

Tears suddenly burned my eyes and I slumped against the wall. If I survived this, I should become a lawyer like my dad and fight stupid laws that gave stupid A.I.R. agents the right to apprehend innocent people.

Never had I felt more violated. More helpless. *At least you acted brave, there at the end,* I told myself. Small comfort now.

What would happen to me next? I wondered. Just how far were these A.I.R. agents willing to go?

With a trembling sigh, I closed my eyes. That proved to be a mistake. My eyelids were heavy, like thousand-pound rocks held them down and there was no opening them once they were closed. The muscles in my shoulders sagged and gradually my chin fell forward. Black spots sparkled through my mind like dark glitter.

How much time passed, I didn't know. I only knew that I drifted in and out of turbulent dreams and hazy wakefulness—and after a while, it was hard to distinguish which was which. I saw flashes of gunfire. Hard, smiling faces that didn't care whether I lived or died. Buildings towering around me, clouds holding me, padded walls.

"She was certainly a surprise," a hard female voice said, pushing into my consciousness.

Still dreaming?

"I know. Came out of nowhere." Phoenix. Like I'd ever forget her commanding timbre.

"How'd she get the wound?" Stranger.

"We're not sure. Somewhere inside the club, though." Phoenix.

"I guess it doesn't matter." Stranger.

You're awake. Have to be. Otherwise you could burst both of those women into flames with a single thought. I kept my eyes closed, my breathing even. Tried not to move even an inch—if I could have, that is. I still felt like lead.

"We had no idea she was working with Erik." Cara. And she sounded bitter.

So. There were at least three people in the room with me. Great.

Cool breath fanned my cheek as one of the girls knelt in front of me. "She's not his usual type." This pronouncement came from the stranger.

Don't frown, don't frown, don't frown.

"And what type is that?" Cara demanded.

"You," the woman replied.

Which was? Pretty? Smart? Both? Everything I supposedly wasn't.

"Well," Cara said, clearly mollified. "That's true."

My teeth ground together.

A pause. Then a tortured "Mia," from Cara. "Do you really think—"

Mia said, "Don't go there. Just shut it, Cara. You dumped him. He's working against us. Don't fall for him again. Look where it got you last time."

Heavy tension filled the room.

Phoenix cleared her throat. "I, uh, pulled up Camille's history. Model student, never in trouble, no hint of being an addict. Parents aren't rich, but they make enough to support her in style. So why would she dabble in Onadyn?"

"Thrills?" Mia said. I heard the rustle of clothing, as if she shrugged. "Love?"

I haven't dabbled in Onadyn, you idiots!

"Not love. Not on Erik's side, at least. For the most part, he ignored her at the Ship," Cara pointed out. "Maybe they aren't working together. Maybe she's a sick little puppy and was stalking him."

"You and I both know that isn't true," Phoenix said. "He knew the minute she stepped onto the fourth floor. You *saw* his reaction to her. His eyes heated; his body language changed, leaning toward her. He was aware of her every move and trying his best not to show it."

What? My heart fluttered.

"But in the end, he did show it." Mia sighed. "You said he gave her something. What?"

"After we cornered them, she told us it was a napkin." Phoenix.

"I searched her and did find a napkin, but it was blank." Cara.

"A decoy, probably." Mia.

There was a second pause, this one so sharp and tight it would have cut me to pieces if I'd moved. Erik had noticed me? His eyes heated when he saw me? Despite the danger, the thought was intoxicating.

"And let's not forget the way he protected her when each of our guns were aimed at her."

"I get it, Phoenix," Cara said hotly. "Point made. You can shut up now."

Strong fingers wrapped around my sore arm. I had to fight back a wince. Cool scissors cut at the bandage and I wobbled in my seat, surprised that I hadn't toppled over yet.

Wait! I was in a seat? Last thing I remembered, I'd been crumpled on the floor.

I took stock: legs under me, butt planted firmly on a flat piece of metal, arms bound behind my back. They'd moved me to the chair and bound me. Dread slithered through me. I was trapped. Totally and completely.

Oh, that sucked. They could do anything they wanted with me and I wouldn't be able to stop them. I wouldn't be able to fight them or shield myself.

Another set of hands settled atop my shoulders, holding me in place.

"What part does she play in this, do you think?" Mia asked. Fingertips probed at my wound.

Relax. Stay relaxed.

"Dumb girlfriend, most likely." Cara. "And it really burns me that he was able to keep her a secret for so long."

"Yeah, but does she sell?" Phoenix clicked her tongue. "What does she know?"

"Well?" Mia said.

Neither of the girls responded.

"Are you just a dumb girlfriend or do you have a solid role in this?" she added.

My dread and fear tripled. She knew I was awake. A part of me expected to be slapped as my eyelids fluttered open. I wasn't. All three women remained in place, staring at me. Frowning.

I gasped when the mysterious Mia came into view. Nothing would be as expected, I guess. Someone with such a commanding voice should have been tall and stocky, even mannish. Not this woman. She was beautiful. One of the most beautiful women I'd ever seen.

She had black hair and swirling blue eyes framed by long black lashes. A small, delicate body. A sweet, angelic face. And yet even bent over me, studying my wound, she looked completely untouchable, removed by emotion and everyone around her.

"Well?" she prompted.

"Not girlfriend," I rasped. "Not seller. Not maker. Not dumb," I added tightly.

"That leaves, what?" Mia pierced me with a fierce stare.

"Innocent."

Cara snorted.

Mia shrugged, as if my answer hadn't mattered. "Someone wanted you dead, little girl. Lancers are used for rendering death, not warnings. An innocent would not have been shot like this. You were doing something you weren't supposed to, weren't you?"

Rather than answer, I said. "I watch the news. Innocents *are* sometimes shot."

The left side of her mouth twitched. Into a smile? A scowl? "So who shot you?"

"The tooth fairy," I replied, not sure where I got my bravado this time.

Mia ran her tongue over her teeth, and I was no longer left in doubt as to whether she smiled or scowled. She scowled at me with potent fury.

Cara stepped toward me, raising her arm with every intention of slapping me as I'd feared. Phoenix held her back.

"I'll tell you what you want to know when my father gets here."

"He's a lawyer," Mia said, a statement not a question.

"Yes."

"He will not be allowed near you *until* you've told me what I want to know. How's that?"

My hands squeezed into fists. "You can't keep him from me."

"I can do anything I want."

"Where's Erik?" I asked, trying a different tactic. *Don't cry. Stay strong. You're brave, remember?* "I want to see him."

"Maybe the tooth fairy will escort you to his cell," Mia replied. She remained where she was, crouched at my side. "Unless, of course, you want to rephrase your answer to my question."

Okay, stay strong but don't talk back anymore. "Let me see him. Please." If they were this forceful with me, what were they doing to him?

Phoenix released Cara and both girls flanked Mia's sides, crossing their arms over their chests and surrounding me with a wall of feminine ferocity. A tremor swept though me. One at a time, they were scary. Altogether, they were hell on earth.

Mia's head tilted to the side as she regarded me intently. "You claim you're not his girlfriend, but you're sure acting like it. Should I believe your words or your actions, hmmm?"

"Words." But she was right. Actions *were* more convincing and all of mine had been damning. "Tonight really was the first time I'd spoken to him."

"Oh, really." Reaching out, Mia tightened her hand around my arm, causing the torn flesh to slowly pull apart. I winced in pain. "I don't want to hurt you, Camille, but I will if I have to. I'll hurt you slowly and often. Got me?"

Suddenly unable to speak, I nodded. The tears that had only burned my eyes a moment ago now spilled over.

"Good. Now." Her grip eased and I was able to breathe once again. "Erik has been transporting Onadyn from the Ship to the public. I want to know how he's doing it without getting caught and I think you can tell me."

"But I can't." With my gaze, I pleaded with her to believe me. "I don't know anything. I swear."

"Are you afraid he'll hurt you if you tell us?"

"Erik would never hurt a girl," Cara said, belligerent.

"Cara," Mia snapped without looking away from me. "Leave."

"What?" The girl's mouth fell open.

"Don't make me repeat myself."

A second passed as shock washed over Cara's face. Then her eyes narrowed on me with absolute hatred, as if it were my fault she'd gotten in trouble. I admit, I did feel a small amount of satisfaction.

I must not have done a good job of hiding it. Hate morphed into rage, tightening her features. She would have attacked me if Mia hadn't stepped in front of me. I jerked back, the corner of my eye catching on the silver tip of a blade. A blade Cara now held. She'd meant to cut me, I realized with shock.

What a violent place this was.

"Cara!" Mia growled. "Last chance."

She flounced from the room, dark hair blowing behind her.

When the door closed, Mia said, "Now then. Camille. You were about to tell me something."

I exhaled a long, trembling sigh. "I can't tell you anything because I don't know anything. I went to the club to see and talk to Erik, maybe dance with him. I didn't know about the drugs until—" Horrified, I pursed my lips together. Damn it! I should not have admitted that. Now they'd grill me for details I didn't have.

"Until," Phoenix prompted, stepping closer.

I looked down at my feet. My boots had been removed,

I noticed. So had my socks. My feet were bare. The blue-painted toenails winked in the light. "Until I sneaked past that guarded door," I admitted. "A group of Ell Rollises attacked me. Erik saved me from them."

"And that's it?" Mia asked. "That's all that happened?"

"Yes."

Mia studied my face for a long while, her gaze deep and probing. "What did he give you? And don't tell me a blank napkin."

"If I tell you anything else, I'll be lying."

"We'll see, little girl. We'll see. I'm going to run some tests on that napkin. And I'm going to interview a few people. Pray they support your accounting." Without another word, Mia strode from the room, the door opening for her automatically.

Phoenix looked from the door to me, from me to the door. She ran her tongue over her teeth in a perfect imitation of Mia, then followed the same path the beautiful woman had taken.

Alone again.

My arm hurt badly. I wanted to go home; I wanted my parents to keep me safe. But more than anything else, I wanted to save Erik the way he'd saved me. If he really was a drug dealer, I wanted to save him from himself. If he wasn't, I wanted to save him from these agents.

Sometimes good people have to do bad things.

Was he or wasn't he? And did it matter to me anymore?

Whether he was selling or not, he wasn't doing it for the money; I knew that. Not when his house was falling down around him. And Erik wasn't a user, a *flyer*. His skin wasn't tinted blue or flaky, two telltale signs.

Did someone he loved need Onadyn?

The thought caught me by surprise and I blinked. Maybe. That was definitely a possibility and would explain so much. If an Outer needed it, but couldn't get it, a dealer could get it for them. But then, that raised the question of just who Erik knew that needed it. A friend? Silver, perhaps?

No. I shook my head. Morevvs were oxygen-tolerant and didn't need Onadyn to survive on our planet.

Who couldn't get it on their own? The poor? Wait. I shook my head again. I think they were given a free supply from the government. Predatory aliens, then? My mouth fell open. Yes. Predatory aliens, those who had been suspected or convicted of a crime, were denied access so they'd have to leave the planet—if they managed to survive being hunted by A.I.R.

Not an easy task, I now realized with a shudder.

Erik could have all kinds of law-breaking friends. Or at least, *suspected* law breakers. I was living proof that A.I.R. sometimes made mistakes. Big mistakes. I was living proof that actions were sometimes misinterpreted.

A holoscreen materialized on the wall in front of me, air dappling like clear jelly. Erik's image appeared on the screen. Seeing him, relief and shock filled me at the same time. He had a black eye, a cut lip, and drops of dried blood on his chin. He'd been beaten, that much was obvious. But he was alive, and that was the most important thing.

Like me, he was tied to a chair.

I watched as Cara stepped into Erik's room, her expression determined. Erik spotted her and smiled wryly.

"Bradley's been notified," she said. "He's on his way here and wants to speak with you."

"Nice move, bringing him in."

"We think so."

Who was Bradley? I hated not knowing. He had to be someone important because a look of sheer torture had passed over Erik's face. A look he'd quickly masked. Had I not been studying him so intently, I would have missed it.

"Trying to break me, Cara?"

"Of course we are, Erik." She paused, studied her blood-red nails. "You deserve to be broken in body and in spirit."

"Well, you'll have to do better than this. I stopped caring what Bradley thinks of me a long time ago. You, too, for that matter." He smirked at her. "It wasn't smart of A.I.R. to send in the ex to interrogate me. I truly don't give a shit what you think of me, babe."

Cara popped her jaw. She turned away from Erik, away from the camera, hiding her expression. "I still care about you, Erik."

"Still?" He snorted. "You never cared about me, or you would have stood by my side when they kicked me off the squad."

She spun around, rage flashing over her face. "You really want to go there?"

"Yeah. Why not? I've got good memories of you sneaking into my cell and—"

"Argh!" She reached out as if she meant to slap him, but stopped herself in time. She backed away from him. Deep breath in, deep breath out. "You're as good a manipulator now as you were then. 'I'm innocent, Cara.' 'You have to believe me, Cara.' " She pounded the wall. "I let you trick me once, but never again."

"Trick you? Whatever you have to tell yourself to sleep at night, babe."

Steps clipped, she paced around his chair. "Why are you acting this way?"

"Because I can," was Erik's response.

"Are you trying to hurt me further? To cut me inside?"

A part of me felt guilty for being part of this intimate conversation. Another part of me eagerly listened, wanting to absorb every detail I could.

"At one time, I would have killed anyone who hurt you," he said. He ran his tongue over his cut lip. "Even myself. Now, I just don't care. You're hurt? So the hell what. Nothing I do to you will equal what you did to me all those months ago."

Once again, she turned away from him. "What do you want from me?"

"I don't want anything from you," he said without emotion.

"Did you expect me to quit A.I.R for you? To plead your case when it was obvious you were guilty?" She laughed bitterly, as if she almost wished she would have had the guts to do it. "That's stupid."

"Yeah, maybe I *was* stupid for expecting the girl who claimed to love me to defend my name." He didn't sound emotionless this time. He sounded torn up inside. "I expected the girl who claimed to love me to believe there was a good reason that I was caught with Onadyn."

"There are no good reasons," she snapped.

He looked away from her, disgusted.

A moment passed while Cara composed herself. She straightened her shoulders, turned, and squared her chin. An air of determination fell over her; she was all business now. "You've been evading us for a long time, Erik."

Slowly he grinned, the action a little mocking. "Is that a big surprise? You're out for my blood."

She waved a hand in dismissal. "We don't care about you; we're after bigger fish. We want to know where the Onadyn is being made. We want to know where it's being stored. We want to know how it's getting to the streets undetected. You give us those details, and you can go free."

"So you can destroy it?"

"Yes."

A muscle ticked in his jaw. "Sorry. You won't get any help from me. Besides, I won't bargain with that information. Ever."

"It kills humans," she said, rage blanketing her pretty brown eyes. "You know that."

"And you know I've never sold it to a human."

"Do I? Your every action screams guilt."

"It saves aliens, Cara. You know *that*, at least."

I was right, I thought with surprise, happiness, and relief. By selling the Onadyn, Erik was trying to save aliens. And they had beaten him up for that? Saving lives wasn't a crime.

"Aliens can receive their Onadyn from proper suppliers like they're supposed to do. Making it, selling it, and buying it without a license is illegal and dangerous. It *must* be regulated."

Erik didn't say a word.

Cara approached him and traced a fingertip across the width of his shoulders. "If you won't tell us about your supplier, we'll beat the truth out of you. And then we'll beat the truth out of your girlfriend."

"She's not my girlfriend," he snapped. Fire blazed in his eyes. "Leave her the hell alone."

*Tsk*ing under her tongue, she sifted her hands through his hair. "You're a liar. Camille's something to you. Oh yes. She is indeed. You're seething with the need to protect the little princess."

"I've only ever told you the truth," he said through clenched teeth, glaring up at her. "She's innocent."

"The Erik I knew would never have involved a civilian."

"This Erik did. I brought her into this when I shouldn't have. That's my bad, not hers."

"Uh-uh-uh. You have feelings for her." Cara's tone was light, but her features were dark, as if a storm cloud covered them. "I can see it everytime you look at her. And I should know. You used to look at me that way. Besides, why else would you have hidden your relationship with her?"

He laughed, and there was genuine amusement in the sound. "A.I.R.'s really getting sloppy if that's what you think."

Scowling, Cara slapped him across the face. He continued laughing. She slapped him again. Blood trickled down his mouth, onto his chin. She slapped him a third time.

"Stop," I shouted at the screen.

"Are you jealous that I'm interested in another woman," Erik said, seemingly unaffected by the violence, "or are you jealous because she's a better person than you'll ever be?"

Plain little me? Better?

Cara paled.

Erik puckered up his lips and made a kiss noise. "Tell Mia she'll have to kill me, because I won't tell you anything about the Onadyn, about the Ship, or about Camille."

Oh, Erik. Don't talk like that. They might take you up on it. My body began shaking and refused to stop.

"We'll get the answers out of you," Cara said, the words drawn, measured.

"Give it your best shot."

Why do they want me to watch this? I wondered angrily. Did they think I'd turn against Erik if I saw him misbehaving? Please. They were turning me against *them* more and more with every second that passed.

"Oh, we will," Cara told him softly. "We won't kill you if we don't get what we want. We'll kill Camille, and you'll get to watch."

8

We'll kill Camille.

They'd do it, too, I thought, my ears ringing loudly with panic. They'd do it without hesitation. Without remorse. Nothing they'd done so far had shown them to be merciful. And let's be honest: Cara would have killed me already if she'd been allowed.

Most likely they weren't even checking out my story. *How can they, Robins? They saw what they saw and that can't be erased.*

The door to my cell opened and my heart almost stopped. Had they come to kill me already?

I heard Cara say, "Convince her to talk to us—the truth, this time." She didn't sound upset or guilty, she sounded smug. "Or, you two can use this time to say good-bye."

The truth. My hands tightened into fists, causing the

laserbands to burn my wrists. "I told you the truth!" I shouted, all of my emotions bubbling to the surface.

Erik was suddenly shoved inside my room. Silent, he quickly caught himself and balanced. Grinning, Cara strode in behind him. Holding a pyre-gun to his temple with one hand, she removed his laserbands with the other.

His gaze locked on me and didn't move. Determination and relief radiated from him. And something else, something I couldn't identify; I only knew it was intense. Hot.

I shivered, growing warm all over. He was alive and he was with me. Finally! It was one thing to see him on a screen, but quite another to see him in person. His very presence comforted me when I should have been puking.

"Why free my hands?' Erik asked. "You up to something?" Silent, Cara backed out of the cell, the barrel of her weapon never leaving Erik. But her features were yearning, needy. She might have betrayed him after he was caught with Onadyn, but she still wanted him. And she didn't like that she did.

Like everyone else in the world, she was helpless against her own emotions.

When she stood in the hallway, the door shut in front of her, leaving me and Erik alone. Immediately he closed the distance between us and crouched behind me. I opened my mouth to speak, but he shook his head. He even reached around and placed a hand over my lips.

"There are cameras everywhere," he said.

"Where?" I asked when he removed the hand. I looked left

and right but didn't see a single one. I'd been filmed without my knowledge. That made me feel all the more violated.

"Everywhere. Believe me. You okay?" he asked.

"Yeah. Still breathing."

"I'm going to rewire your bands. This may—"

"Ow!"

"—sting a bit," he finished. "Sorry."

I'd felt a jerk, a burn, but I was now free and no longer quite so helpless. Pulling my arms into my lap required a conscious effort. They were shaky and weak and the skin around my wrists was red and inflamed.

Moving hurt, but I twisted in the seat to face Erik. Seeing his cuts and bruises in person, those badges of pain and suffering, was like being stripped and placed in front of a hose blasting ice-cold water.

What had they done to him, to cause his eyes to blacken and his lip to split like that? He was strong, yes, but even the strongest of men could be killed. "Are *you* okay?"

He smiled wryly, then winced. He dabbed at the side of his lip, taking away a fresh bead of blood. "I'm better than ever."

"Liar," I said without heat.

He chuckled. "Caught me."

"Erik—" I said at the same time he said, "Camille—"

Despite the dire circumstances—or maybe because of them—we laughed, taking amusement where we could it, before lapsing into silence.

"You first," he finally said.

"I told them the truth, but they want to *kill* me. We've got to—"

He placed his hand over my mouth, effectively cutting off my next words. I eyed him with curiosity. He freed my mouth but didn't pull away. His fingertips traced the curve of my jaw and I shivered. Nerves, I assured myself.

"They're listening to everything we say, which is the only reason they allowed me inside your cell." He didn't try to quiet his tone but spoke loudly. "I used to work with them, here in this very building, so I know their tricks. They want us to talk, to reveal our secrets."

I guess he truly had been an agent. He was strong enough, don't get me wrong, and he was smart enough. But in my mind, he was still a high school student who strutted down the halls, who joked with Silver, and flirted with all the (socially visible) girls.

"Understand what I'm telling you?"

"Yes."

"Good." He'd released my bands, yeah, but with his words another wave of helplessness bombarded me. Constant surveillance was the same as being tied down. No way we could escape—and I desperately wanted to escape.

"Don't worry," he added. He dropped his hand, but not before he allowed his fingers to linger, to trace the seam of my lips in an act of comfort. "Everything's going to be fine. I promised."

Silly of me, but I wanted his hand back on my face. His

touch was all the things I remembered: warm, callused, soothing. Besides Erik, no boy had ever touched me like that. I liked it; I wanted more.

"I'm sorry I accused you of selling to humans."

Eyes narrowed, he cracked his jaw. "I take it they let you listen to my conversation with Cara? And you believed me?"

"Yes. And yes."

"Some people would say selling Onadyn to aliens is as bad as selling to humans," he said loudly, and his tone left no doubt that he thought those people were idiots.

"Why would they do that? If it saves lives?" No one deserved to die like the alien I'd seen in that photo.

"Good question," he muttered. Then sighed.

Gathering my courage, I said, "I can see why you'd want to leave this line of work," for the benefit of those listening, as well as to lighten Erik's dark mood.

"Yeah, and why's that?"

"Not only do the living conditions suck, but your former coworkers are assholes." There. Take that, ladies! A.I.R. would not defeat me. And I would not cower. Not anymore.

Who are *you?* my mind demanded. *Have you been taken over by an Outer?*

Erik slowly grinned. "I like you more and more, Camille Robins. You're a sound judge of character."

I returned his grin. I liked him more and more, too.

"I'm sorry about the napkin," he said. "I shouldn't have done that to you."

Maybe I imagined it, but as we smiled at each other, some sort of tension sparked between us. Not a bad tension. A needy tension. I wanted a kiss, needed a kiss. Did he? My heartbeat quickened and fire spread through my veins. *People are watching,* I reminded myself.

I cleared my throat. "So as an agent, did you ever have to kill anyone?" A topic A.I.R. already knew well, I'm sure.

"Yes." A faraway glaze slithered over his eyes. Dark memories sunk deep claws inside of him, pulling him down a terrible spiral. "I was recruited on my eighteenth birthday."

"You don't have to tell me this, if you don't want."

He continued as if I hadn't spoken. "I was out celebrating and had too much to drink. Got cocky. Rude. Insulted an Outer. We fought. Not an easy, push-away fight, either, but a bloody, violent fight that broke several of my ribs, sliced my stomach, and fractured my wrist."

"Wow."

"An agent saw the entire thing. My opponent, you see, was an Arcadian, one who could move faster than the blink of an eye. I managed to hold my own and even inflict some damage, something most humans wouldn't have been able to do." He shrugged again, none too casually this time. "A.I.R. took me from the hospital the next day, bandaged me up, and began training me to become an agent. A killer."

I smoothed the hair from his forehead, realized what I'd done, and jerked my hand into my lap. "Those girls . . ."

He nodded stiffly and stood. His boots had been removed,

as well, I noticed, leaving him barefoot. "Yep. Kids taken from high school and trained to become A.I.R. agents. We trained together."

I wanted to stand, too. Maybe lay my head on his shoulder and wrap my arms around him. He sounded so sad. But I remained in place. Any more touching, and they'd think we really were boyfriend and girlfriend. They already thought I was a liar; that would just add fuel to the fire.

"Why'd you leave?" I asked.

He massaged the back of his neck. "You heard. I was caught with Onadyn."

"Yeah, but there's got to be more to it than that. They seem to, well," I hesitated. "I'm sorry to say this, but they seem to hate you. Being caught with Onadyn is a crime, yes, but I don't think it's worthy of such hatred."

His gaze was sharp as it leveled on me. "You hated me when you first found out. Don't try to deny it."

"I'll deny it if I want." I stubbornly lifted my chin. "I didn't hate you. I was disappointed in you and shocked. But even then, I had a hard time reconciling what you were saying about yourself to the boy I'd built up in my head. I mean, look at the way you took care of me."

His eyes widened in surprise and he shook his head as if he couldn't quite believe I'd said that out loud. "You truly amaze me, Camille Robins."

He meant it; I could hear the truth in his voice. No boy had ever said anything like that to me. A few that I had dated had told me I was pretty—to get into my pants. But to be told that I amazed someone? And said in a tone that dripped of reverence and awe, and not to get into my pants? Never.

"Thank you."

"You're welcome." He backed up a few steps, turned, and braced his hands on the wall. The back of his shirt was ripped and I could see fat red welts peeking out from beneath the torn material.

"They whipped you?" I gasped out.

He didn't face me. Didn't answer me. Just continued his story as if we'd never veered off track. "I met Cara about a month after I'd been accepted into the camp. We hit it off right away and started dating."

I hadn't asked, but I'd wanted to know. Badly. So I allowed him to ignore my query without protest.

"We had a pretty intense relationship for a year and spent every spare minute together. And when we weren't together, we were thinking about each other." He turned around and stared at the wall opposite him, as if he wasn't speaking to me but to whoever was listening to our conversation. "I loved her."

"You were eighteen?" My age now.

Erik nodded. "Yep."

My dad would say a kid that young couldn't possibly love with such passion, that teenagers had no concept of "true" devotion. A crush, he'd say. A passing fancy. *You'll wake up tomorrow and realize you never really cared about that guy,* Dad always said when he'd caught me sighing over Erik's picture.

Dad was wrong.

I hadn't gotten over my crush on Erik. I felt as intense about him now as I had then. My dad didn't understand—or perhaps he didn't want to admit—that teenagers experience emotions as violently as adults. Perhaps more so, since the feelings are new to us and we haven't yet learned how to deal with them.

When Erik said he'd loved Cara, I believed him. The truth was there in his expression, glowing brightly. He'd loved her, had probably wanted to spend the rest of his life with her. Would probably have died for her.

To have a boy love you that much, well, it had to be empowering. I was jealous, I admit it. I didn't like Cara, and didn't think she deserved him.

"What happened?" I asked quietly.

He gave a bitter laugh. "The day I was caught with Onadyn happened. Apparently A.I.R. had suspected my involvement with the drug. They sent Cara in to search. She found it and didn't even ask me about it. She just fucking turned me in. I was cuffed and taken to Mia, where I was questioned and found guilty."

"I'm so sorry."

"Cara, too, was questioned. She betrayed me faster than I could draw in a breath, claiming she'd suspected it all along, too, that she'd stayed with me to get proof."

I ached for him, for the bitterness he still harbored. Such a betrayal had to have destroyed him, ripped him up inside.

"I was jailed. Cara came to visit me, crying. But it was too late. I stole her badge and managed to escape. I hid for a little while, even bleached my hair and permanently changed my eye color. I wasn't doing anybody any good, though. So I changed my last name and joined your school. I knew A.I.R. would find me eventually, but I didn't care. There was something I had to do, consequences be damned."

He lapsed into silence leaving me—and our audience—to wonder just what he'd had to do. "And were you able to do it?" I asked.

"Not yet. But I will." There was determination in his voice. "Lives depend on it. Many lives."

Whose? His? Or someone he loved? Probably the latter. He sold Onadyn—a crime that had destroyed the life he'd built—to save aliens. Not many people would do the same.

I probably wouldn't have, I was ashamed to admit.

"We don't have a lot of time," he said with a sigh. "They'll grow tired of our conversation soon enough."

And when they did, they were going to kill me.

How could I have forgotten, even for a moment? Just like that the cell seemed to crumble around me. *Stay calm.*

"How's your arm?" Erik asked.

"Hurts a little." No reason to deny it. I'm sure my usual sun-kissed skin was pale. My eyes might even have been blood shot. I needed sleep. Real, safe-in-my-bed sleep. I needed more of that numbing paste. Most of all, I needed assurance that we'd find a way out of this.

Erik approached me and knelt between my knees. He cupped my cheeks, forcing me to face him. I drank him in, concentrating on him rather than reality. His dark eyes, with their long, spiky lashes, mesmerized me. His full, pink lips—lips that would have been pretty on a girl but somehow made him all the more masculine—enthralled me. The wide set of his shoulders enveloped me.

Concern blanketed his features as he studied me.

"I'll be okay." I hope.

"I'm proud of you," he said. "You're injured, but you haven't broken down. You could have run away, but didn't. You've never experienced anything like this, but you're holding your own."

"Th—thank you." I felt like a weak link and here he was praising me some more.

"You were questioned, I imagine?"

I nodded, guilt staining my cheeks. I tore my eyes from his and gazed at his shoulder. After everything he'd told me, I hated to admit that I'd told A.I.R. some of what he'd informed me of in the car.

In a way, I'd betrayed him just as Cara had.

"How'd it go?" he asked.

Sighing, I let the entire episode pour from me, leaving out no detail. He didn't stiffen as I expected, didn't curse at me or even scold me.

"You did good, Camille," he said, surprising me. "A trained agent couldn't have done better."

"But—but—"

"A lot of times, people make up stories, telling their tormenter what they think he or she wants to hear. That gets them into trouble because they can't remember the little details and end up changing their story, which makes them look even guiltier. You stuck to the truth, you didn't elaborate, and you didn't let their threats sway you."

More praise. Wow.

He traced his thumb over the seam of my lips, exactly like he'd done before. Only this time, he lingered. His eyes darkened, heated. I experienced another of those delicious shivers.

I didn't compare to Cara in looks, I knew that. Even that woman, Mia, had known it. But Erik was peering at me as if I were exquisite. I was probably dirty, definitely had wrinkled and bloodstained clothing, but he didn't seem to care.

"I'm sorry for the way I treated you at school," he said. "I'm sorry for ignoring you."

I nibbled on my bottom lip, moistening the trail of fire his thumb had left behind. "That's okay."

"No, it's not." He gave my head a little shake and his hands tightened around my jaw. "You deserved better than that."

My heart hammered inside my chest. Not from pain. Not anymore. And not from fear, which I should have been feeling as time continued to slip away. I felt wild and excited and eager.

Kiss him, one part of me said.

He might reject me, the other part replied.

Uh, hello. Are we looking at the same boy? He won't reject you. And so what if he does? Nothing ventured, nothing gained. You're brave now, remember?

A.I.R. will think you lied.

They already do. Well, decision made.

Without asking permission, I leaned forward and gently pressed my lips to Erik's, careful not to hurt him. I didn't care who was watching, who was listening, or what they thought of my actions. There was only here and now. Only Erik. Only a kiss . . .

Wonderfully, his head titled to the side, angling for better contact. His tongue slid into my mouth, hot, touching mine, tasting. Tingles moved over my skin, warm and drugging. One of his hands tangled in my hair and our tongues thrust together harder, faster.

His spicy male scent enveloped me, drowning me in everything that was Erik. Blood rushed through my veins, awakening feelings that I'd never experienced before. A need to go further, all the way to the finish line. I didn't want to die without experiencing sex. Without knowing all of him.

Delicious, I thought. *Wondrous.*

More.

Slowly, however, he pulled away. His breathing was labored and so was mine. I kind of expected A.I.R. to burst inside the room, guns blazing. But a moment passed, and they didn't.

"Did I hurt you?" I asked softly, eyeing the cut on his lip.

I ran my tongue over my own lips, taking in the moisture he'd left behind.

"It was worth it," he said, his voice low, husky. His eyelids were at half-mast and he gave me a soft, sweet (too quick) kiss. "I wanted to do that the first time I saw you."

My face scrunched in confusion. "At the club?"

"No." He shook his head. "At school."

I laughed, surprised that I was able. "You didn't even know I was alive until today."

"We already covered this. I did notice you."

That's right. He had. Slowly I lost my grin. "Why did you ignore me, then?"

"My first day at school, I was shown around the building. Do you remember?"

"That doesn't answer—"

"Hear me out."

"Fine. Yes. I remember." I'd been at my locker, talking with Shanel, and he'd passed me. First I'd caught a glimpse of pale hair and then my gaze had dropped to his jean-clad butt. As if he'd sensed my scrutiny, he'd turned and our eyes had locked. I'd felt the air seep right out of my lungs.

"You were with your friend and you were laughing about something," he said. "A laugh that was uninhibited and completely free. Made me turn around. And when I saw you, your cheeks were rosy, like now, and your hair had come undone from its pins, framing your pretty face."

Pretty? Me?

He smiled wryly. "I wanted to be the one to make you laugh like that, to put that color in your cheeks. But I had a mission and I couldn't lose sight of that. You would have been a distraction I couldn't afford so I pretended you didn't exist."

"I—" Didn't know what to say. I tore my gaze from his, staring down at his chest. Where his shirt gaped, I could see the black cat tattoo. He'd noticed me that day. He'd really noticed me. Not just the necklace, but *me*.

All this time, I'd thought I was invisible to him.

"I don't want to die," I whispered. I needed to experience more of his kisses.

"I know. I don't want you to die, either."

"What are we going to do?"

A long sigh slipped from him, fanning my nose. He leaned toward me and placed a soft, lingering kiss on my left cheek, then a soft lingering kiss on my right. "We're going to escape," he whispered. "We're going to escape."

9

There were no windows, no doors that I could see. Not even a visible seam in the wall, where the agents had come and gone so freely. Yet I knew the door was there. I just didn't know how we were going to get it open.

Erik must have read the confusion on my face because he smiled and whispered, "Trust me."

I did, I realized. I'd come to trust him. Everything he'd said about A.I.R. had been true. "I do." He'd worked here. He knew the ins and outs, knew the players we were up against. Escape, though, wouldn't prove easy. We were under intense scrutiny, our every move monitored.

"Thank you." He kissed me again, a swift meshing of our lips that rocked me to the core. When he pulled back, he was grinning and I was breathless.

I watched as he straightened and paced in front of me, left, right, left, right. The cell was small with nothing that could be used as a weapon. The only piece of furniture was the chair I sat upon and it was made of steel and anchored to the floor.

We needed a miracle.

I recalled how Shanel had once wanted to be an alien—no, not once, I realized. Earlier today. Wow. Seemed like a full year had passed since we'd driven to the Ship and my entire life had changed. She'd wanted superpowers, mind-control powers, something, *anything*.

For once, I wished to be an Outer, too. Who cared if you were taunted? Who cared if you were considered ugly? As long as you could protect yourself, as well as those around you, nothing else mattered.

"You able to walk?" Erik asked me. He scratched his ear and flattened one hand against the wall.

"I—think so." I hurt everywhere now and weakness beat through me with heavy fists. But I'd force myself to walk to the end of the Earth if needed. Erik trusted me to do my part, and it was time I proved I *was* strong.

"Good." He paced to the other side of the cell, scratched his other ear, and once again flattened his palms against the wall. "What about running? Think you can run?"

If he'd given me time to respond, I would have asked why he was speaking so loudly since A.I.R. was listening. But he didn't. He dove on top of me, knocking me out of the chair and onto the cold, hard ground. I lost my breath, struggling to suck in air as his weight pinned me.

Boom!

A loud, screaming explosion rocked the cramped space. Metal chips and chunks of debris rained all around us. Even on top of us. A large piece slammed into Erik's back and he hissed through his teeth.

Seconds later, an alarm screeched to life.

The air grew thick and black with plumes of smoke. I coughed.

"Stay low to the ground," Erik said. He rolled off me, grabbed the wrist of my injured arm, and jerked me into a crouch.

I winced, instinctively trying to pull away.

He eyed me in confusion, realized what he'd done, and gave me a quick smile. "Sorry." He wrapped his fingers around my other arm and tugged me forward. "This way. We don't have much time."

Somehow he'd managed to blow up an entire wall, presenting us with a wide opening. We crawled over metal and rock and into an empty, smoking hallway. Again, I coughed.

Erik stood and helped me do the same. I swayed and he wrapped an arm around my waist. The floor was cold on my bare feet.

"There should be agents out here," he muttered.

We trudged forward and rounded a corner. "Where'd you get the explosives?" I asked as we moved. Bits of debris dug into my heels, but I didn't let it slow me down.

"The man I work for demands that all of his employees

wear flesh-colored explosive tape behind their ears. It's virtually undetectable. Until it's too late," he added with a grin.

My mouth fell open in horror. "What if you'd blown yourself up?" If I had the tape, I would have been terrified of such an occurrence. And I might not have approached him or even gotten within a hundred yards of him if I'd known he wore it. I certainly would *not* have kissed him!

"Couldn't have blown myself up. The tape is made of a chemical that doesn't become active until it comes into contract with a certain metal—the very metal A.I.R. is comprised of."

Okay, wow. Ingenious.

"What I want to know is where all the agents are," he said.

Yeah. Me, too. He was right. It was weird that they weren't here. Phoenix, Mia, and Cara hadn't seemed like the type to let us waltz out of here without a battle royale. "Do they *want* us to escape?"

He frowned. "They're idiots if they do, but in all the years that I've known them, they've never *let* someone walk out the door. Something had to have happened. Something big to draw their attention away from us."

After several twists and turns, we raced down another hallway. How Erik knew where we were going was a mystery to me. All the hallways looked the same. Silver, nondescript. Ominous.

"The computer should be shouting our identities and what

sector we've breached," he said, "but the ID scans are off." He sounded confused. "Why would they turn the ID scans off?"

He wasn't speaking to me, I knew, so I didn't bother trying to answer.

Each time we came to a small, black box on the wall, he popped open the top and jerked out some of the wires. "That should keep some of the agents from following us, if they ever get their asses in gear."

A door slid open at the far end of the hall and two agents appeared. They'd gotten their asses in gear, I guess. They pounded toward us, guns raised. But there was surprise in their eyes, as if they hadn't expected to see us.

Erik shoved me to the side and rushed them. I stumbled and hit the wall with a yelp, watching as he ducked and kicked out his leg, knocking the agents together before they could squeeze off a shot. One fell on his side and dropped his gun. The other fell but maintained a strong grip and finally fired.

A yellow stream of fire slammed into the wall, just above Erik's ear.

Erik jumped on top of the man and the two rolled on the ground, punching each other. Only then did the weapon skid a few feet away. Both men were fluid and lethal with every blow, going for the groin, the trachea. But they were both good at blocking, as well.

Should I try and help? Or would I hinder?

No time to think about that now.

I watched, wide-eyed, as the second gunman rose and

shook his head to clear the dizziness. He scowled as he searched for his weapon. Adrenaline rushed through me, giving me strength, and I sprinted forward. Yesterday I would have run in the opposite direction. Anything to avoid danger.

Today I ran toward it, wanting to protect Erik the way he'd protected me.

The agent beat me to the gun, but his attention was focused on Erik as he aimed.

"No!" I shouted, drawing his gaze.

He swung at me and I ducked the way I'd seen Erik duck. I kicked out my leg, trying to trip him. Unfortunately the guy didn't topple as he'd done for Erik. He did waver, though, and that gave me the opportunity I needed to throw myself at him. We flew backward. He twisted us midair so that I took the brunt of the fall. On impact, I sputtered and gasped for air.

The guy rose to his knees and aimed the gun at my chest. My mouth dried in fear but I didn't stop fighting. I hadn't escaped my cell to die here. Acting instinctively, I jabbed my fist up and into his nose, rolling as I did it in case he fired.

He hissed and did, indeed, fire.

The beam nearly hit my shoulder, but ended up singing the ends of my hair instead. An ashy, sickening scent filled the air; I struggled to my feet. A second later, the guy screamed. Erik was there, right behind him, kicking him in the stomach and knocking him down.

Only when the guy was writhing in pain and holding his

side did Erik grab the gun. He tugged me to my feet. "If he follows us . . ." I said.

"He won't. Kidney shot. Gets them every time," he told me. Then, to the man, he said, "Where're your friends?" He aimed the gun, barrel pointed at his heart.

"Morevvs," the agent said through clenched teeth. "They've attacked the outside of the building."

Silver, I thought, wide-eyed. How had he known we were here? Erik and I shared a glance. "Tracking device," he said, answering my unspoken question.

Invisible explosives. Tracking devices. There was a world around me that I'd never known existed. Until today, I hadn't cared.

Several more agents appeared at the end of the hall, but Erik quickly fired the pyre-gun, making them dive for cover. We took off in a dead run.

When we reached the end of the hallway, he disabled the ID box, once again twisting the wires and fusing them back together in different locations. "Most criminals don't know how vulnerable A.I.R. is because of their ID system," he explained. "It's a well-guarded secret and was one of the first things we learned at training camp, so we'd be prepared if we were ever locked out because of it." As he spoke, he jumped up and pounded at the ceiling.

"Keep watch," he told me and handed me the gun. "If anyone comes toward us, fire first and ask questions later."

My hand shook, but I aimed down the empty hallway.

Waiting. Waiting. Thankfully, no one came. But I did hear them pounding against the metal door. Heard a motor of some sort, as if they were trying to saw their way through.

"If I open the door, we'll be faced with about one hundred armed and pissed agents," Erik said. He continued to beat at the ceiling, bits of plaster falling at our feet. "So we're going to move through the vents."

"Vents?" Tiny, confined spaces, trapping us like rabbits? *Don't panic, don't panic.*

"Well, they aren't really vents. They were put here in case agents needed to evacuate without going out the front or back doors."

After he'd pounded a large enough hole for us to crawl through, he jumped and grabbed the edge, then hoisted himself up. He reached down, took the gun, and offered me a hand.

Using my uninjured arm, I reached up. My fingers intertwined with his, and he hefted me beside him. "Thank you," I said, the words echoing. Trepidation consumed me. The space was small, tight. Dark. "Won't they know where we are when they see the hole?"

"By the time they get here, it'll be too late. Now stay behind me, okay? And stay quiet."

I nodded.

He crawled forward and I remained close behind him. My knees were raw and I wished to God I'd worn pants instead of a skirt. The vents seemed to get smaller and darker the higher we climbed. At least there was a breeze of cool air so I didn't feel confined or trapped. Still, my legs and arms began to burn from exertion.

Below me, I could hear footsteps pounding and agents yelling at each other. The alarm had quieted, thankfully, so that no longer echoed inside my mind.

What seemed an eternity later, Erik stopped. He held up his hand for silence—as if I would have dared speak or even breathe—and listened. My eyes finally adjusted to the dark and I could see his profile, hazy though it was. Strong nose. Shadowed beard stubble, and a firm jaw, clenched as he concentrated.

I listened, too, but heard nothing.

He turned left and motioned for me to follow. I did. We reached a dead end. I didn't have time to panic. He jerked a vent cover from the wall, producing a new opening. He dangled his legs over the side, holding onto the edge to keep from falling. But then, to my surprise, he released his grip and disappeared. I heard a gentle tap as he landed.

"Camille."

I inched forward and peeked through the opening. Erik stood in a dark, spacious room. Alone. There were beds, one after the other lined against each side of the wall.

"Jump," he said. He held up his arms and motioned me down with his fingers. "I'll catch you."

I shook my head. The drop wasn't bad, but it was still a drop and I'd already been battered and beaten enough for one day. Besides, I didn't want to hurt him. Some of his cuts had opened and blood trickled down his bottom lip and chin.

"Jump."

No other way, Robins.

"Jump!"

Oh hell. "You'll catch me?" I didn't think my legs could hold my weight. "What if I hurt you?"

"I'll catch you. And you can't hurt me."

With a sigh, I wiggled until I was sitting with my legs through the hole. Holding my breath, I let myself fall. My stomach nearly rose into my throat. Erik caught me as promised, as if I weighed no more than a bag of feathers. He settled me on my feet, kissed me quickly, and raced to the window.

Had I not grabbed onto one of the bed rails, I would have fallen. As it was, my knees wobbled and I struggled to remain upright. "Where are we?"

"This is where agents sleep when the night is quiet and uneventful. And since there's chaos below, I knew no one would be here." He aimed the pyre-gun and squeezed the trigger. No sound, only heat. The glass-like material melted, dripping liquid crystal onto the bottom frame.

Plumes of smoke wafted, but the outside air wafted inside, pushing them away and dancing my hair around my face.

Erik removed his belt and anchored the middle on a thick wire just beyond the seal. "Come here," he said without looking back at me.

I moved toward him as fast as my feet would carry me—

which wasn't fast. "I don't like this," I said, already suspecting what he wanted me to do.

He tugged on each side of the belt, pulling them taut. "You want to live?" Finally he faced me, peering at me intently.

"Yes."

"Then put your arms around me and hold tight. And do not let go for any reason. Understand?"

"Yes," I repeated. Dread filled me.

He stepped onto the ledge and I joined him, shaking uncontrollably. We were higher than I'd realized. Or anticipated. Below us, lights zoomed and flickered over the ground, highlighting a violent battle already in play. Agents were going toe-to-toe with aliens. Morevvs. Some were fighting with their fists, some were fighting with guns. But the Morevvs, I noticed, were moving away from the building.

"The Morevvs are going to disappear soon, leaving the agents free to come after us." Erik's tone was as dark as the night. "The longer we stay here, the smaller our chances of success."

Without another word of complaint, I wrapped my arms around his neck as commanded. "I'm not scared," I lied. "I'll be fine."

"Don't scream." In the next instant, Erik jumped.

I bit his shoulder to keep from screaming. He hissed in my ear, but didn't ask me to stop. Down, down, down we glided, his belt our only anchor. I expected it to snap at any moment. Excepted us to drop and splat on the concrete like bugs against a windshield.

When we landed, I was jostled to the bone and almost fell flat on my face. Erik gave a rough jerk, keeping me upright. Someone spotted us and fired. A blue stun beam whizzed past my shoulder. I finally screamed.

That, of course, drew more attention. Several more rounds of fire launched at us. Yellow, this time. Fire.

"Run!" Erik shouted, tugging me into a mad dash.

We raced into a blackened alleyway, where other buildings stretched on each side. He cast a glance over his shoulder. Frowned. "No one's following us. That really was too easy."

Too easy? Too easy! We'd almost died. We'd jumped from a building without a parachute or landing mat. We'd been shot at.

He threw another frown over his shoulder. We reached a well-lit patch and golden moonlight bathed his face, lit his eyes. "They'd love for me to lead them to my boss. Maybe . . ."

"Still not see anyone?"

"No. But that doesn't mean they aren't there." He cursed under his breath and rounded a corner.

I panted, doing my best to keep up. "Maybe leading A.I.R. to your boss isn't such a bad thing, Erik."

"You don't know what you're talking about," he snapped. "You have no idea what will happen if that man stops making Onadyn."

"I just—"

"No. You don't understand."

"Then for God's sake explain it to me."

He opened his mouth, closed it. Opened, closed. Finally, he changed the subject. "Listen. Ryan Stone was fighting the Morevvs, and that's one point in our favor. Believe me when I say that he's not the kind of guy you want to meet in a darkened alley. He'll beat the shit out of both of us just for giggles."

"How is that a point in our favor?"

"When he's in town, he and Phoenix are inseparable. She wouldn't have followed us without him."

I relaxed. A little. "What should we do?" Now that we were out of that building, my adrenaline rush was fading. My arm was hurting worse than ever and the weakness in my limbs was spreading. I was still shaking. My feet throbbed as twigs and rocks beat against them.

I wasn't used to this kind of life and knew I couldn't last much longer.

Erik flicked a third glance over his shoulder. "Damn it, this doesn't feel right." He ground to a stop and looked around.

Panting, I leaned against the brick wall. "Since we're taking a moment, why don't you tell me why it would be such a bad thing to destroy an illegal Onadyn ring. I know you want to help Outers, but other people are surely using that Onadyn to sell to humans. And if we help A.I.R., they might leave us alone."

"I won't bargain with them. Yeah, they might leave us alone," he said, raking a hand through his hair, "but other people would die."

"Explain."

For a long while, he didn't speak. Then he sighed and said, "The aliens who need it will stop getting it." Pause. "See, a while back, I chased a predatory alien into an alleyway very similar to this one. He was suspected of beating a human to death. We questioned him, found him guilty, and killed him. Then, because I'd been the one to catch him, I had to be the one to tell his family what had happened."

Guilt and pain dripped from Erik's voice. A part of me wanted to tell him to stop talking, that I'd heard enough. But I sank to my knees and motioned for him to continue. He needed to get it out and I needed to know the truth. "What happened then?"

"He had a wife and two little kids and they were devastated. Sticking to procedure, I instructed them to leave the planet."

"Did they?"

"No." He laughed bitterly. "They couldn't return, they said, because their planet was in ruins. There was nothing left and they would die there. But you see, they were going to die if they stayed. They were not oxygen-tolerant. And, linked to a predatory alien as they were, they could no longer get their supply of Onadyn. They couldn't afford to buy black market, either."

Erik's features glazed with fury, obliterating the guilt but not the pain. "They'd done nothing wrong," he said, "but they were being punished."

"That wasn't your fault, Erik. You were doing your job."

"My job could have killed them." He slammed a fist into the brick wall. "I visited them a few days later and they were near death already. Two little kids, Camille, unable to breath because of me. Me! You should have seen them. Writhing. Groaning. Contorted."

"Erik."

"Have you ever seen someone die from lack of Onadyn?"

"No, but I've seen pictures of the end result."

"That's nothing compared to *watching* it happen." Scowling, he punched the wall again. "I was determined to save those kids from that kind of fate."

My respect for him deepened.

"I'd investigated an Onadyn dealer who we hadn't yet proven guilty and approached him. He refused to sell to me, thinking I meant to bust him. I—I stole it from him and took it to the kids."

"I'm glad," I said, meaning it. Of course he'd taken the kids Onadyn. He cared about people, about innocents. He would not have allowed them to die, no matter what he'd had to do.

It had taken courage to do what he'd done. It had taken honor. And it had taken determination. He had to have known he'd lose everything. But he'd done it anyway. I told him all of that.

Erik peered over at me in surprise.

"You did the right thing," I said. "I understand now. I do.

139

And I agree with you. That family should not have been punished for their father's sins."

He turned his gaze to his feet. "I came to District Eight because I knew Silver's dad was selling Onadyn illegally. I'd heard about him from another agent, but I'd never met him. I worked my way into his life and bought the drug from him until I ran out of money. I didn't know what else to do, so I started selling it for him to pay for what I needed. I didn't know what else to do," he repeated.

"I wish I had the guts to do something half as brave."

Quicker than the blink of an eye, he moved in front of me. He cupped my jaw and planted a swift kiss on my lips, a kiss that was hard and soft at the same time. "You're braver than you give yourself credit for."

I met his stare. "And you're more honorable than you give yourself credit for."

His grip tightened. "I've never sold it to humans. You have to believe me. I've only ever sold it to aliens who needed it but couldn't get it on their own. My goal has always been to learn how to make it myself and set up my own lab."

"I believe you. But you don't need your own lab, Erik, you just need to change the law." The words came out of my mouth, but they were straight from my dad. He loved working and manipulating the legal system almost as much as he loved me and my mom. Never for aliens, though, always for humans.

That needed to change, I decided.

Erik snorted.

"No, I'm serious. It can be done," I said.

He shook his head and stepped away from me. "That takes time, and these people don't have time." He held up his hand to silence me when I opened my mouth. "A.I.R. already knows where Silver lives, so going there won't give them any information they don't already have. Can you make it?"

I nodded. No way I was staying here, so close to A.I.R.

"Then let's go. We'll figure out our next move when we get there."

10

Panting and sweating, we ran for over a mile. Always we remained in the shadows. Always my heart beat like a war drum. Somewhere along the way—between looking over my shoulder for the thousandth time and praying God struck me with lightning so the night would end—I tripped and scraped my knee, ripping my new, cool syn-leather skirt (not to mention my pride).

"You've had enough," Erik said between heavy breaths. He eyed the nearest street, left and right, then withdrew a black velvet pouch from his pocket. He crouched in front of a blue four-door car. "Let me know if anyone drives by."

"O—okay." *I guess being his lookout makes me an* official *criminal,* I thought, scanning every shadow, every hollow, every building. "Where'd you get that?"

"From one of the agents." Unrolling the velvet produced

142

two thin, scalpel-type objects. He cut the plastic ID pad in the center, digging a deep hole, then rewired several of the lines. "Accept new voice," he said. "Start."

The car roared to life.

"Open."

The driver-side door opened.

Grinning, he ushered me inside and then claimed the programmer's seat. He keyed in Silver's address and we eased onto the road. All the while, he (and I) watched for any sign of A.I.R. They never appeared, thank the Lord, and soon we reached the Morevv's mansion perched on top of a hill.

A rainbow of pale pinks, yellows, and blues, the house seemed to pulse with energy. Trees and roses flourished throughout the manicured lawn. They were fake, those trees and blooms, since Mother Nature had been decimated during the Human-Alien War so many years ago and had yet to replenish herself properly.

And yeah, the war between humans and aliens was now fought privately. Something I hadn't known until tonight. I'd assumed we were living in harmony and at peace with our visitors. I shuddered. What a fool I'd been.

The car eased to a stop at a towering iron gate. Erik placed his left palm in the ID box. Blue light instantly glowed and scanned each of his fingers, lingering on his thumb.

Finally, a computerized voice said, "Welcome, Erik."

The gate slowly creaked open. Obviously Erik had done this before and was a welcomed guest. My heart, however, pounded with uncertainty as the car inched up the long, winding drive.

"I just thought of something," I said, straightening in my seat. Dread coursed though me. "Shanel and Silver."

"Yes?"

"Will they be picked up by A.I.R.?" Just the thought caused bile to burn in my throat. And yeah, guilt. I hadn't thought about her or worried about her as much as I should have.

Erik reached over and squeezed my hand. "Your friend is fine. Silver would have called me if they were being chased."

"Unless he was incapacitated."

"He's not incapacitated. He sent those Morevvs for us, remember?"

That's right, he had. I relaxed. Slightly. "Silver might be okay, but that doesn't mean Shanel is. A.I.R. could have picked her up at home."

We reached the front entrance of the house and the car stopped. Erik didn't exit, but shifted in the seat and faced me. He studied me intently, silently. Then he said, "After you passed out at my place, I called Silver and told him to keep Shanel with him. She's fine."

Every muscle in my body slumped. "Thank you."

"You're welcome." Erik manually exited. Around he raced and popped open my door, holding out a hand.

I had to use every ounce of my strength to stand. My knees wobbled and almost gave out, but he kept his arm around me and held me steady. Morning was fast approaching, painting the sky in a haze of pretty hues, and the air was hotter, wrapping me in a warm cocoon.

Safe, I though. *Finally.* That was all my body needed to prepare for sleep. My eyelids drooped heavily and exhaustion pounded through me. A thin fog wisped through my mind.

Obviously informed of our arrival, Silver opened the French double doors and pounded down the porch steps. His blue hair blew around his shoulders as his gaze took in our ragged, bloody appearances. "Glad to see you alive."

Erik grinned. "Thanks for sending in the troops to get us out, man."

"My pleasure," Silver said. "I would have sent them sooner, but didn't think to track you until later."

The two guys slapped each other on the shoulders, jostling me. "Where's your dad?" Erik asked.

"Hasn't made it home yet."

Erik motioned to me with a chin tilt. "Tell Camille her friend is okay."

"She's fine," Silver said to me. "She's inside and sleeping peacefully."

Even though Erik had assured me that Shanel was fine, hearing it confirmed was like waving a magic wand of relief over me. "Thank you. Thank you so much for keeping her safe."

Erik's arm tightened around my waist as he ushered me inside the house. The smell of plants and dirt wafted to my nose. Not a bad smell, but a little strange. He didn't say a word as he led me up the marble staircase, past alabaster vanities and colorful art. Past plush red rugs and crystal holoscreen TVs. There was even a chandelier with hundreds of lights that looked like dripping stars.

"Where are we going?" I asked. Were my words slurred? Even to myself I sounded far away, as if I stood in a tunnel. I wanted to see Shanel and tell her what had happened to her car.

"You're going to bed. You're barely able to stand."

"But—"

"No buts. You can talk to Shanel in the morning. She'll probably be pissed about the car, and I don't want you to have to deal with that now. You've been through enough."

I thought about arguing, then pressed my lips together. I'd reached my limit and we both knew it. "Okay."

"I stay here a lot, so they keep a room ready for me." He stopped at an azure metal door with a swirling design etched around the frame. "This is mine."

After a quick hand scan, the door slid open. We stepped inside and I gasped. Colorful murals decorated the walls. My eyesight was too hazy to make out all the details, just a rainbow of shades. A large bed with black silk sheets consumed the center of the room. A small rock waterfall pressed against the far end, emitting a peaceful rush of smooth, dappled liquid.

A soft black fur rug—that was probably illegal to own—was draped over the floor. I didn't know which animal species.

Most animals were on an endangered list; quite a few had died during the war with the Outers.

"Wow," I said.

"I know. I didn't do the decorating, but it suits me."

"Me, too."

Erik kissed my temple. "There's a shower to the right and clothes in the dresser. Use anything you want. I'll be in the room next door if you need me. Shout, and I'll come running."

"Okay," I said with a chuckle, gazing longingly at the bed. Sleep. How wonderful that sounded. Thirty minutes ago, I hadn't thought I'd ever sleep in a bed again. I'd thought I'd be sleeping with corpses for all eternity.

"Don't hesitate to call for me," Erik said firmly. "I mean it."

I nodded. Erik lingered, watching me with tenderness and concern in his eyes, but he finally left. I remained in place for a long while. Here I was in Silver's house. Alive. With Erik seeing to my every need. Who would have thought I'd find myself in this position? Sure, people were chasing me. Sure, my parents would freak if they knew where I was. Sure, I'd almost died. That hardly seemed to matter at the moment.

With a sigh, I trudged forward. The bathroom was bigger than my entire bedroom at home, with a silver-veined marble floor and chrome faucets. In the back, beside the toilet, was a command box. I punched the button for the shower and a dry enzyme spray began shooting from several nozzles.

My limbs were shaky as I stripped and removed my bandage. The wound looked better than before, less red, less angry. Already scabbing. I stepped into the center of the shower, letting the spray cleanse me from inside out. The dirt and blood and sweat that had caked me dissolved instantly. Hmmm. A shower had never felt so delicious.

I'd heard the wealthiest people in the world bathed in hot, steamy water. I think I would have preferred that, searing rivulets beating against my sore muscles, but oh well. I'd take what I could get.

Finally clean, not a speck of grime on me, I padded to the dresser and pulled out a white T-shirt and a pair of boxer shorts. Both were big on me but they were soft and comfortable. I was wearing Erik Troy's clothing. Someone pinch me. Or shoot at me. Or slap me around. I snorted. Been there, done that.

Unable to stand a moment longer, I fell onto the cool sweetness of the mattress. Erik's spicy scent enveloped me, wrapping me in a sense of safety. Sleep claimed me in the next instant.

———

Drugging warmth surrounded me as surely as Erik's scent. Delicious warmth, welcomed warmth. "Hmm," I muttered under my breath, trying to wake myself up.

There was a heavy weight pressing into the curve of my

waist, but even that was something to be enjoyed. I wanted to linger in bed forever. But a nagging pain in my arm insisted I wake up.

Sleep a little longer. So warm. So comfortable.

Yes, just a little longer. No. Not longer. Ow. Ow, ow, ow. Take a pain pill, Robins!

My eyelids fluttered open, soaking in the bright light of the bedroom a little at a time. The walls were multihued, not the plain gray of mine, and boasted of frolicking fairies and blooming forest murals. Where was I? Why did I hurt? I frowned.

I stretched my good arm over my head and arched my back—and hit something solid. Frown deepening, I rolled over, unsure of what I'd find. My injured arm screamed in protest and I squeezed my eyes closed. Deep breath in, deep breath out.

As the pain subsided, I opened my eyes and once again faced the world around me.

Every cell in my body froze the moment I spied what I'd hit.

There, beside me, was Erik. Sleeping soundly.

Instantly all of last night's events flooded my mind. The shooting, the car chase . . . the kiss . . . being locked up, escaping . . . the kiss . . .

Had we . . . *no,* I thought then. We hadn't. I would have known and Erik would not have taken advantage of me like that. He was too honorable. I knew that all the way to my bones. But more than that, I suspected he was desperate for someone to trust him, to believe in him, as no one in A.I.R. had done. Each time I'd mentioned that I trusted him, he'd given me a look of utter astonishment. And hope.

No, he wouldn't have betrayed that. Much as I probably would have liked it.

I reached out and brushed a stray lock of pale hair from his forehead. How peaceful he appeared. How relaxed. Like a little boy, not a hardened man. I was kind of glad he was asleep. I'd never woken up next to a guy before and didn't know quite how to handle myself.

"Good morning," he said, his voice a sleep-warm purr.

I yelped in surprise. Not asleep, after all.

Chuckling, he slowly opened his eyes. Brown irises rimmed with black lashes peered at me. He rubbed a hand down his face, wiping away the sleep. "How's your arm?"

"Hurts." His ease helped relax me and I softened into the mattress.

"A little more paste and it should heal up nicely. How'd you sleep?"

"Like the dead." I hadn't even felt him climb into bed. "I thought you were sleeping in the other room." There was no heat in my tone. Despite my surprise and slight nervousness, I was glad he was here.

"I was. You must have had a nightmare, because you were tossing and turning and crying for help."

Hope I hadn't said anything embarrassing. "Sorry."

"I was happy to help," he replied with a warm grin.

I couldn't help but return the smile with one of my own. He was just too sweet. Too cute. Too mine. For the moment, anyway. *Kiss him.* I bit my bottom lip. I couldn't kiss him with morning breath. Ugh. "Will you excuse me for a moment?"

His brow puckered in confusion, but he nodded.

"Don't move. I'll be right back." I lumbered from the bed, cringing when my bruises throbbed. I stumbled into the bathroom, where I searched until I found a toothbrush. There were several new ones, the disposable kind, still in their boxes. I picked the green one, opened the package, and brushed my teeth, all the while checking my appearance in the mirror. My hair was tousled, wild, and there were shadows under my eyes.

"Good as it's going to get," I muttered. There, on the counter, were all the supplies I needed to fix my arm. Erik must have set them out for me. I applied the numbing paste, the stinky cream, the cooling gel, and finally the bandage. My lips inched into a smile.

Ah. Sweet relief. No pain. I could concentrate fully on Erik. And kissing him. Practically vibrating excitement, I exited and stepped back into the room.

Erik was not on the bed as I'd left him. Where had he gone? My excitement mutated into disappointment. A second later, however, he strode from the side door. I lost my breath. He looked good. Really good. He'd cleaned up, like I had, and now wore a pair of jeans, the adhesive strip unfastened. No shirt.

His skin was bronzed, ripped. His tattoo stretched over his stomach, his belly button acting as one of the cat's eyes. Was it bad that I wanted to pet that cat?

When he spotted me, he ground to a stop. His gaze became a dark inferno. I didn't speak as I walked to the bed and lay back down. He did the same. We faced each other, not touching. Just *knowing*. I could feel the blood rushing through my veins, an awakened river.

I didn't want to let fear rule my life anymore. I didn't want to be a coward and not do the things I wanted most. And right now I wanted to kiss Erik Troy.

Right now, I wanted everything he had to give.

Still silent, I leaned toward him. As it turned out, I didn't have to say anything. He met me in the middle. Our lips meshed, both opening automatically. Our tongues thrust together and his warm, minty flavor danced across my tastebuds.

One of his hands tangled in my hair, pulling me so close our teeth banged together. His other hand wrapped around my waist, trailing heat up and down my spine. Delicious heat.

I flattened my palms on his chest and his tiny nipples speared me. I could feel the quickness of his heartbeat. His skin was hot, so hot. Burning. Our bodies pressed together— mmm, I wanted to arch and moan, *did* arch, *did* moan—and then he was rubbing against me.

Hot before. Blistered now.

I panted his name. "Erik. Erik."

"I'm right here, baby." He cupped my breast, kneading.

I gasped in surprised delight.

"I want to make you feel good," he said.

"I do. Promise." I continued to arch forward, back, forward again, unable to stop the actions. Moaned again. So badly I wanted to reach between us and feel him, really feel him, that part of him that made us different. I didn't, though. Too unsure. Hadn't done that before, didn't know if he'd like it. If I'd do it right.

Where's the brave girl who kissed him?

"Erik?"

Someone said his name and it wasn't me. That barely registered in my brain, however. More kiss. More touch. More. Just more.

"Erik? You up, man?"

Who was—?

"Erik?"

Erik stiffened and pulled away from me. His breathing was ragged. He pressed a button on the black box perched on the nightstand. "Yeah, Silver. I'm up."

"Breakfast will be ready in fifteen."

My gaze locked with Erik's. His expression tightened, the fine lines around his mouth straining. "Thanks." He pressed the button again.

Several minutes passed and neither of us uttered a word. I used the time to get myself under control. Breathing—slow, easy. Skin—cooling degree by degree. Hunger—stubborn, remaining.

"I, uh, should probably call my parents," I said. Now there was a sobering thought. "I need to let them know when to expect me." And that I'm okay, in case A.I.R. had finally contacted them.

Slowly Erik frowned. "I don't know, Camille. You're in deep now and your parents could be used against you." He pondered it for a moment. "What did they think you were doing last night?"

I sat up and shook my head, hair tumbling down my back, tickling. "They thought I was staying the night with my friend, Tawny."

He relaxed against the pillow. "All right. Call them and tell them you want to stay another night with Tawny."

"But I don't really have a friend named Tawny," I admitted, biting my bottom lip. "Shanel and I made her up so we could stay out all night. I didn't worry about them trying to call her so late at night, but they might try to call sometime during the day."

Erik regarded me for a heartbeat of time before bursting into laughter. "Hard to picture you lying to Mommy and Daddy."

"I know," I mumbled. "I'm a menace."

"You keep this up and you'll soon be picking fights and taking names."

I rolled my eyes, but I'd be lying if I claimed I didn't like the image. Me, kicking ass. Oh yeah.

Erik's serious edge returned and he said, "You can't go home yet, Camille. A.I.R. will be watching your house, waiting."

Sighing, I rubbed my temples to ward off a sharp ache. "They could have contacted my parents already, who could be worried sick about me even now."

Once more he scrubbed a hand over his face. "Having worked for A.I.R., I know how they operate. They'll refrain from worrying your parents so that you're less afraid to go home. They might secretly tap the lines, yeah, but not worry the parents."

"Still . . ."

"If you want, you can call them and tell them, I don't know . . . you're running away or you need time to think about your life. Or if you want to stick with the truth, tell them A.I.R. is chasing you but that you're hiding and you're safe and you'll call them again in a few days. Keep it brief, though. Sound good?"

My stomach rolled at the thought of confessing what I'd gotten myself into. They'd be worried (if they weren't already), and they'd be disappointed, and they'd be pissed. They'd demand that I come home right away. But maybe . . .

I blinked as an idea hit me. Maybe my dad could help Erik and his cause. Maybe my dad could work the system and help change the laws so that aliens could receive Onadyn when they needed it, no matter who they were related to. Dad had never worked on behalf of Outers nor for their needs, but if his only "precious" daughter begged him to do it . . .

"I'll call them," I said, determination rushing through me.

Erik reached behind him and grabbed a cell unit from the

nightstand. He placed it in my hands, but didn't pull away. He lingered, tracing my fingertips with his own. "I'll give you some privacy," he said, and there was a wistful edge to the words. "I'll check on breakfast. You, me, Silver, and Shanel will have a big, long talk. Okay?"

"'K. Hey!" I groaned as something else occurred to me. "Why doesn't A.I.R. just storm *this* house?" I asked, my nerves now all the more raw.

"This house is actually owned by a human—or a human identity, I should say. Aliens are smart, and have learned to get fake IDs just as humans have. They find a child who died, take the name, have all sorts of legal documents drawn up, and then . . ."

Would I ever learn the ins and outs of this life?

He shrugged. "A.I.R. has stormed this place several times before, but always came up empty. Now a lawsuit is pending. They can't enter again without absolute proof of wrongdoing. And if they tried, we'd be notified and out before they ever hit the front steps."

No, I wouldn't, I decided.

"Kitchen's down the steps, past the living room. First room on the right." He rolled from the bed.

I could have stared at him all day. He was so strong, capable, and sure. My gaze landed on the welts on his back. Crap. I'd forgotten about them and had rubbed him there. Maybe squeezed. He might be strong, but that didn't mean I should abuse him.

"Did I, uh, hurt you when I, uh, kissed you?"

He glanced at me over his shoulder and smiled. "Totally worth it."

A blush heated my cheeks.

He left the room without another word, the door shutting behind him automatically and cutting him off from my view. A sense of emptiness hit me.

Sighing, I looked down at the phone. "Here goes," I said with trepidation, then spoke my dad's name and address into the mouthpiece. The phone dialed immediately and I almost threw up. Almost disconnected. In the end, I was a brave little solider and remained on the line. Barely.

My mom finally answered, breathless, as if she'd run to the phone.

"Have you talked to anyone about me, Mom?" were the first words out of my mouth.

"What? No. Camille?" she asked, clearly confused.

Before I could stop myself, I told her how I'd lied about Tawny, what I'd done, where I'd been, and what had happened. At first she laughed like I was joking.

"Listen to me and hear the fear in my voice. Everything I've said is true. A.I.R. *is* chasing me." After everything I'd done to presereve my lies, admitting the truth felt surprisingly good.

There was a pause. A gasp. A whimper. She began to believe. There was terror in her voice as she yelled at me. The disappointment I'd anticipated came next as she cried.

"I'm sorry," I said, feeling lower than I ever had before. "So very sorry, but it's safer this way. For everyone. I have to go now."

"Camille!" Her panic stayed my hand and I didn't disconnect. "Don't do this. Come home." Desperation clung to every word, all the more potent because of the panic.

My stomach churned. How could I do this to her?

"We'll sit down together and discuss this," she said. "We'll find a way to get you out of this situation. Everything will be okay. You'll see. We'll call the police. We'll have your dad call the district attorney. They're golf buddies. You don't need to run or hide."

"You didn't see the way A.I.R. treated me." And now that I'd escaped them, making me appear all the more guilty, they'd be even worse. "If the police were to give me back to them. . . . Tell Daddy to start looking for ways to change the Onadyn laws," I said with a trembling breath. "If Outers aren't predatory, they should be allowed to get the drug no matter who they're related to. Kids are dying, Mom, and we have to do something."

"Camille. Camille, sweetheart, listen to me. I need you—"

"I really have to go now. I love you, and I'm sorry. Stay safe." I hung up before she could say another world. Before she could talk me into forgetting what needed to be done. A tremor rocked me from head to toe.

I couldn't believe I'd just confessed such crimes to my mother. Things might never be the same between us again. But that was okay. I wasn't the same girl I'd been.

Tossing the phone aside, I clumped from the bed. My legs were shaky, but not as bad as before. I changed into another of Erik's shirts. Instead of boxers, however, I pulled on a pair of gray sweatpants and tied them at the waist. He'd also found me a pair of boots and had placed them by the door. I tugged them on—but not before I'd smothered the cuts and bruises with that numbing paste.

When I was done, a quick glance in the mirror showed that I didn't look my best in the baggy clothes and the dark circles of fatigue hadn't faded from under my eyes, but I didn't look my worst, either. I looked fragile, delicate. And yet, I looked ready to take on the world. Determined. My cheeks were rosy, my lips slightly swollen.

I look kissed, I thought.

Smiling, I trudged from the room and managed to find the stairs without losing myself in the maze that was Silver's house. My stomach growled in anticipation of a meal. I smacked my lips, only then realizing how dry my mouth was.

At the bottom of the stairs, I heard laughter and familiar voices and followed the sound, smile growing again at the thought of being with Er—uh, Shanel. Shanel! I quickened my steps and bypassed the very comfortable and expensive-looking living room with its overstuffed chairs and polished wood (real?) floors. As Erik promised, the kitchen was the first room on the right.

Erik, Silver, and Shanel were seated at the round table, drinking juice and nibbling on syn-eggs. My mouth watered. I inhaled deeply, savoring the mouth-watering scent. How long had it been since I'd eaten?

An alien woman—an older, beautiful Morevv—stood at the stove, frying something blue, I realized. With scales? Ugh. Okay, I wasn't so hungry for *that*. Whatever it was. The woman herself was a pretty pink color from head to toe.

Sensing me, Erik glanced in my direction. He smiled. "Everything okay?"

I nodded. Yeah, it was. My parents now knew the truth, but I could live with their upset because I'd done the right thing.

Shanel faced me and squealed. She clapped her hands and jumped to her feet. "Camille! You're here, you're really here!"

We raced toward each other, meeting in the middle, and hugging. She still smelled like dirt, and in that moment it was the best smell ev-er. Her soft red curls tickled my cheek.

"Tell me everything!" she said. "Erik is being secretive."

"Are you okay?" First things first. My gaze raked over her, noting that she appeared healthy and whole and glowed with rosy happiness. Sadly I had learned that appearances could often be deceiving.

"I'm better than okay." A wicked twinkle sparkled in her emerald eyes. "When Silver and I left the club, we came here. He had to talk to some people about helping Erik—speaking of, I'm upset with you for not telling me good-bye at the club, but I'll forgive you because Silver told me you got sick and—hey, are you all better?" She didn't wait for my response, but continued, "Silver and I talked and laughed and played cards and Rose—" Shanel pointed to the Morevv at the stove. "—the housekeeper, made us cake and we ate it and it was so good."

"Uh, babbling much?" I said with a laugh. But my laughter quickly faded and I gripped her forearms, holding her steady. "Your car," I gulped, mentally fortifying myself to confess. "A.I.—"

"Cops," Erik interjected. "Cops."

Whoops. "The *cops* have it. I'm so, so sorry. They were chasing us and caught us and cuffed us and hauled us downtown."

She paled, freckles standing out. "My dad is going to kill me."

"Erik told me about the car last night," Silver said. *"My* dad is already working on getting it back."

Slowly the color returned to Shanel's cheeks. "Thank God," she muttered.

"I truly am sorry, Shanel."

"It'll be all right, Camille. Really. If I have to, I'll tell my dad that that bitch Tawny stole it."

My relief was so intense, I laughed. And I don't know why, but my gaze sought Erik's. He was watching me, his brown eyes warm. Everything inside me heated as I mentally replayed what we'd done earlier. The kiss, wandering hands, straining bodies.

"You little tramp," Shanel whispered, watching me watch Erik. "Did you sleep with him?"

"Yeah," I answered in that same whispered tone, tearing my eyes from Erik.

"I knew it! How was it? Tell me everything. I'm so jealous!"

"We slept." Would I have done more if we hadn't been interrupted this morning? I didn't know. Okay, I did know. Yeah. I would have. Eagerly. Happily. "I swear we didn't do anything except sleep, though."

Disappointment clouded her features. "That seems to be the way of it in this house, no matter how hard you try."

"So you and Silver didn't . . . you know?"

She shook her head, red curls flying. "I wish."

"What are you two whispering about?" Silver asked in his deep, rumbling voice.

"Nothing," Shanel told him, then skipped back to the table. "Just girl stuff."

I followed her and Erik kicked out a chair for me—the one beside him. The Morevv housekeeper, Rose, walked over and placed a platter of that scaly blue stuff on the table, then left us alone.

"What *is* that?" I asked.

"Brentaes. They're like fish, only they don't live in water and they come from my planet," Silver answered. "My father brought the animal with him when he came to Earth and has raised and bred them ever since." He scooped some onto his plate. A fine string of slime stretched from one plate to the other. "It's good. Try it."

I looked at Erik. He nodded and mouthed, *Try it.*

Great. No help there. Not wanting to offend the host, I tentatively reached out and pinched a section of the brentaes between my fingers. Firm. Warm. A little grainy. Slowly I placed the square into my mouth. I chewed. My brow wrinkled. Not bad, I realized. "Tastes like chicken."

Erik laughed.

Shanel tossed a piece at me and it left a trail of slime down my shirt.

Silver rolled his eyes.

That's when Silver's dad strode into the room, whistling under his breath. He was wearing that half-mask; his metallic gray eyes (hadn't they been amber last night?) glowed brightly. I'd been reaching for a piece of syn-bacon so I could throw it at Shanel, but I froze, hand poised midair.

He spotted me and stopped. His gaze then took in the rest of the scene. How comfortable we were with one another. How at ease we were in the house. Well, not so at ease anymore. Everyone sat completely still, completely silent, waiting for his reaction.

"The guards told me the four of you were here, but I assumed you would still be in bed. Heard you held your own last night. Sorry about your arm," he told me. He snatched a few pieces of syn-sausage and left.

O-kay. I'd kind of expected him to attack me. At the very least, threaten me again.

Erik drained a glass of juice, unconcerned, as if there'd never been anything to worry about. "I've already told Silver everything that happened. He wants to protect his dad and the . . . product." He glanced meaningfully at an oblivious Shanel—who must not know about the Onadyn. "Which means he needs to help us."

"What product?" Shanel asked. Nope, she didn't know. She heaped her plate with food. "And help you with what?"

Yeah. With what? Escaping A.I.R.?

Erik explained bits and pieces of the situation, omitting all references to Onadyn and A.I.R., claiming there was a misunderstanding with a group of boys from our school. When he finished, Shanel clapped happily and cheered about what an "adventure" this was.

Had I once been so naive?

Silver had the opposite reaction. His expression hardened with every second that passed. Obviously one of the reasons he and Erik were so close was that they both felt the same way about Outers who needed Onadyn but couldn't get it through legal means.

"I've got to run to the bathroom," Shanel said, popping to her feet. "Want to come with me, Camille?"

I shook my head, content to stay with Erik.

Pouting slightly, she said, "Don't say a word until I get back," and flounced off, a flash of red.

"There's something you should know, Camille," Erik said a moment later. He paused and dread washed over me. "Silver's a half-breed. He's part of two different alien races: Morevv and Arcadian."

I think my jaw hit the floor. "That's—that's impossible. Right?"

"I assure you, it is possible. It's simply not talked about. Scientists deny it, agents deny it, though a few suspect. At camp, I even heard rumors that Mia Snow was a half-breed, part human, part Arcadian. And I know some of my other instructors were aliens of some kind, whether they were full or half." He shrugged.

Mia's face flashed into my mind. Flawless skin. Exquisitely arched eyebrows. Small nose. Silky black hair, and eyes so blue they were unfathomable pools. Almost, dare I think it, otherworldly.

Alien and human. Wow. Just wow.

"I need Onadyn to live," Silver said. "Which was why my dad makes and sells it. He doesn't want me to be dependent on the government for my survival. Not when that support can be taken away in the blink of an eye, leaving me helpless."

Erik reached over and laced our fingers together. "Silver's one of the reasons this mission is so important. Silver and others like him. Before I take you any further, I need to know that you're in this until the end. No matter what."

I didn't have to think about it. I nodded. "Of course I'm in this until the end." I only hoped the end came later rather than sooner.

"Good." He nodded. "I've been mulling this over and here's what I think we should do . . ."

11

"Are you sure this will work? What if it doesn't?" The words poured from me as I stared out the window of our car, other vehicles whizzing past us. It was midmorning on a bright, sunny Sunday, so everyone in the world was out and about, it seemed.

Erik flicked me a patient glance. "It'll work. I wouldn't put you in any more danger than necessary."

"Don't take your eyes off the road!" I gasped out. He was driving Silver's Jag manually, which scared the crap out of me. When the computer was in charge, the turns and stops were smooth. When Erik was in charge, I was jerked forward and backward repeatedly.

"This *will* work."

We were supposed to divide A.I.R., half following us, half following Silver and Shanel because it was easier to lose a half rather than a whole. The downfall: There could be another car chase and I didn't think my heart could take it without bursting a few vessels.

Silver lining: Death might be okay now.

Another downfall: We'd been at this for half an hour and we hadn't yet lost our tail.

Yep, the minute we'd pulled out of Silver's drive, A.I.R. had made their presence known. They hadn't rushed us as I'd feared, but had remained a safe distance behind, letting us know they were there without encroaching on our space.

I wondered if Silver and Shanel were having any luck.

"Maybe it's time to try something else," I said. I didn't like being this close to those agents. Deep down I knew they probably were hoping we'd lead them to the Onadyn. Otherwise they would have busted into Silver's house and arrested us. Still. They could change their minds at any moment and attack.

"Maybe you're right." Erik sighed. "We *have* to lose them because I have to get to the warehouse. I should have made an Onadyn delivery this morning, but . . ."

He didn't have to finish. But. Yeah. We'd run into a lot of those lately. "You know, if I had known my trip to that night-club would turn out this way, I still might have gone," I said to distract him, to distract myself. "Can you believe that?"

"Yeah, I can. I think you're a closet danger junkie." He increased our speed and jetted off the highway and onto a service road. Several cars honked. Ours bounded up and down and swerved. "I wish the night had ended differently for you, though."

"Hey, I met my objective, so I guess I can't really complain. I got you to notice me."

"Hell yeah, I noticed you. I noticed you the moment you stepped onto my floor. You've got the sweetest legs I've ever seen and I could hardly take my eyes off them to do business. Even when I spotted Cara, I could only think about you."

Pleasure bloomed inside me. "Really?"

"Really."

I grinned; I couldn't help myself.

"Get ready for a bumpy ride." He yanked the steering wheel left and we turned sharply.

I lost my smile and gripped the edge of my seat, sweat beading over my skin. *Stay calm. Don't think about it.* Soon the road became gravel, and then the gravel disappeared altogether, leaving only dirt.

A fence appeared several yards in front of us.

"Uh, Erik." He wasn't slowing down. He was speeding up. "You're going to hit—"

We rammed into the fence, knocking it over the top of the vehicle. I yelped. Trees appeared in every direction, tall, green, their branches scratching the metal car doors. I'd driven past this place several times and knew it was a government-protected forest, a place where oaks were being grown and nourished.

"Unbuckle," Erik commanded.

Unbuckle? Uh, no. Not even for a million dollars.

"Unbuckle."

"I'll fly through the window if you crash."

"Unbuckle," he repeated, harshly this time. "We're going to stop, jump out, and run like hell. And don't even think about arguing again. Our other option is to jump out of the car while it's still moving."

Dear Lord. The trees thickened as he maneuvered left and right, right, right. My mouth dried. "I understand," I managed to tell him. My hand shook as I unbuckled the only thing that would save me from slamming into the windshield if we crashed.

As promised, the car screeched to a halt without hitting anything. Immediately Erik opened the door, not waiting to command it to open, but shoving it open himself. I was a little slower, but was soon at his side. He clasped onto my hand and we raced into the dense forest.

I thought I heard the hum of another car, the slam of a few doors. Then my ragged breathing filled my ears and *that* was all I heard. Towering bark and leaves whipped past us. The thick foliage overhead kept us in welcome shadows and the scent of dirt and dew saturated the air.

I hope he knows what he's doing.

"Don't worry," he panted as if he'd read my thoughts. He tossed me a wicked grin. The guy loved danger, apparently. "I know exactly where to take you."

Ten minutes of running and my lungs started burning. Fifteen, and my legs started shaking. "I can't go much farther," I wheezed.

"We're almost there," he said between breaths. "You're doing great. I'm proud of you. You can do it."

The pep talk helped. *Yes, I can do this.* I *would* do this. I pumped my arms harder, pushing myself onward.

We came to an electric fence. I hunched over to suck in a great gulp of needed air, watching as Erik removed his cell unit from his pocket. He hooked the thin black box to the fence, careful not to let his skin touch the wires. There was a spark, then another. A few seconds later he said, "We're good to go."

Uh . . . what? "How?"

"The cell unit is specially designed to absorb and disable any electrical output." He was already climbing as he explained. He stopped, reached out, and offered me a hand.

I took it, allowing him to hoist me up.

Once we hit solid ground, he reached through the holes in the fence and removed his phone. We maneuvered through back alleys and around crumbling buildings. An eternity passed. Soon there were raggedly dressed people wandering the sidewalks, others leaning against the walls and drinking from liquor bottles.

I kept throwing glances behind me to make sure we hadn't been spotted. So far I hadn't seen anyone suspicious, hadn't seen any familiar faces.

Finally Erik stopped in front of a peeling blue door. Hand scan. A pop. He shoved open the wooden door—not metal as most were made of, I noticed—and jerked me inside. *Drip.*

Drip. I could hear the slow fall of water droplets from somewhere in the building as Erik used a piece of timber to block the door.

"I know we lost them in the woods," he said. "We're safe now. We'll stay here until nightfall, then head to the warehouse."

"Call Silver and make sure he and Shanel are okay." I placed a hand over my heart, hoping to slow its frantic beat.

He shook his head and pounded forward, into the small but well-stocked kitchen. "Not yet. I don't want to distract him if—" He pressed his lips together and refused to finish.

If they're being chased, I mentally finished on my own. They weren't, I assured myself. They were safe.

As a distraction—I seemed to need those a lot lately—I glanced around. "What is this place?" There was a black couch, two chairs, a TV, and a table and stove. All the comforts of home. And yet it appeared forgotten. Not lived-in. Dust painted every surface gray and musky. Specks even glinted in the air.

"This is one of my safe houses," was the response. He grabbed two bottles of water from the fridge and tossed one at me.

I caught it and quickly drained the contents, transported to heaven as the cold liquid rushed through me, cooling me down. *One of,* he'd said. Lord, how many did he have? "I seriously hope your former buddies don't know about it."

Erik turned and leaned his back against the refrigerator's frame. "They don't. I made sure of that." Drinking, he strode to the far wall and placed his palms at the bottom of the left corner. Another hand scan—which amazed me since I couldn't see an ID box on the wall—and other *pop*. The wall split down the center and slid apart.

"Sweet baby Jesus." A large computer screen, several keyboards, and many things I didn't recognize came into view, all pulsing with different colored lights.

"The entire building is monitored twenty-four hours a day, seven days a week." A stack of papers caught his eye and he bent down, picking them up. He straightened, frowning.

"What is it?"

"I keep these here as a reminder. See, I was too late one night," he said, as if in a trance. "A woman died."

I could hear the pain and self-deprecation in his voice. "I'm sorry."

"*This* is what happens if I fail."

My throat tightened. "May I see them?"

He glanced over at me. "Sure you want to?"

I nodded and held out my hand. Slowly he stretched out his arm. I drew in a breath and claimed them, then drew in another and closed my eyes. *You can do this.*

Finally, I looked.

The images were as horrific as the photos I'd seen in my dad's office. An Arcadian female was doubled over, her expression one of frozen agony. Her fingers were curled unnaturally, her elbow bent at an odd angle. Her skin was tinted red, vessels having burst beneath the surface.

"There are hundreds of them in need of the drug," Erik said. "Maybe thousands."

"You can't save them all." Guilt swam through me. I'd never even tried to save one.

"But I can try," he replied softly. He wheeled one of the chairs to the keyboard and punched in a series of numbers.

Beside me, I heard another *pop*. I set the photos aside and spun around in time to see another wall split, this one showcasing three tiers of guns, knives, and other killing devices I didn't want to contemplate.

My mouth fell open.

"At A.I.R. training camp, we learned to be prepared for anything," he explained.

"War, from the looks of it."

Erik chuckled. "War, definitely." There was a heavy pause and he lost his air of amusement. "Don't freak out on me, but we're going to have to alter our appearances. I've got the necessary supplies in the bathroom." He flicked me a glance. "You'll look good Goth. Promise."

I nearly choked. Me? Goth? "That'll make me stand out even more."

"Yeah, but people quickly look away from the extreme."

"You sure?"

"Sure. A.I.R. isn't looking for Goths. They're looking for an average, dark-haired guy and a beautiful brunette."

My mouth fell open at his words. He kept saying things like that, calling me sexy and now "beautiful." No wonder I was so hot for him.

As if he hadn't just rocked my world, he punched a few more buttons on the keyboard. "Ever handled a pyre-gun before? And I don't mean holding one or grabbing one from an assailant—or a friend," he added with a frown, clearly thinking of the time I'd grabbed his and pointed it at Cara, "but actually firing it."

"Uh, no."

"Want to?"

"Sure." Might be fun. Not.

"Pick one."

Wait. What? "Now? You want to start target practice *now*?"

"Yeah." He nodded. "No better time."

"I—I—okay." *Please don't let me kill myself or Erik,* I silently prayed.

He stood and closed the distance between us. Hands on my shoulders, he spun me around, facing the weapons. He smelled familiar, good, like pine and sunshine and that spicy scent that was all his own.

His body heat enveloped me, reminding me of this morning, of our kiss, but I didn't allow myself to shiver. He'd notice, probably ask me about it, and I'd have to admit that I couldn't get his kisses out of my mind.

Remaining behind me, he reached over my shoulder and palmed a silver gun. The crystal perched between the barrel and the handle winked in the light. With his free hand, he positioned my fingers at the right angles, but didn't let the gun near me. Yet.

"Be careful of my arm," I said, because I was nervous and didn't know what else to say.

"Always," he replied, and then the cool steel was pressing against my skin.

I jumped. I don't know why.

"Easy," he said, fitting me and the weapon together. He kept his hands over mine. "Good."

"This is lighter than I expected." In fact, if I closed my eyes I could pretend my hand was empty.

"The metal is special, but all pyre-guns are made so that they don't melt while spitting fire."

I wouldn't have to worry about burning my fingers when I pulled the trigger.

"Aim for me."

I stretched out my arms, aiming as commanded.

Erik twisted me so that I was aiming at a wall, not his other weapons. I could feel the muscles in his arms and chest bunching with each movement.

"Fire it," he said.

"No. No way." I shook my head for emphasis. I'd burn the entire building to the ground.

"Fire," he repeated firmly.

"But—"

He closed his finger around mine and squeezed the trigger.

A yellow beam shot from the tip of the gun, propelling forward, slamming into the far wall. I nearly screamed and had to bite my tongue to hold the sound inside. There was no recoil, though, just smooth and easy-as-breathing stillness.

Didn't matter. Hello, freak out. "I just fired a gun."

"The lower half of the building is comprised of the same metal as the gun, just like the A.I.R. building. Nothing will melt it."

"But the front door looks like it's made of wood."

"It's *painted* to look that way so no one will suspect the truth."

I glanced from the weapon to the unaffected wall, then back to the weapon. He was right. There wasn't even a hint of smoke or ash. "You said A.I.R. is made of this stuff, too. How did you burn that window then?"

"Windows are different. That's why I removed them for the lower half of this building."

I hated that I didn't know this stuff already. Cara did. She was strong and confident. *So are you. Now.* Still. Did Erik compare us?

He didn't speak as he removed the gun from my grip and replaced it on its velvet holder. He didn't speak as he turned me around to face him. He didn't speak as he cupped my chin in his hands and forced me to meet his gaze. "You stiffened. What's wrong?"

A sigh slipped from me. "I'm not war-savvy. Usually I'm the biggest coward around. The past two days, I've been stronger and braver than I have my entire life, but I still don't compare to your friends."

"Former friends." His hands tightened on my jaw. "I've told you how well I think you've handled yourself throughout this entire ordeal and you haven't had a single day of training. Not to mention the fact that you're injured. And you might not know about weapons, but that doesn't make you any less of a warrior. You've pulled through this like a champ. I've told you that before and it's time you started believing me."

I hated to admit this—oh, how I hated it—but my bottom lip quivered and tears burned my eyes. God, what was wrong with me? He was saying such nice things. No reason to cry. "Look at me," I said, wiping the tears with the back of my wrist and sniffling. "I'm acting like a baby."

"That's because you're exhausted, running on adrenaline and grit. That will topple anyone, including me."

"I don't think anything could topple you." I looked at him through the watery shield of my lashes.

He grinned. "Once, I was out on assignment, stalking a group of predatory Mecs. They were controlling the weather so it was hot and dry. I had to stay in that heat for six days while I tracked them, never really able to rest because I was afraid I'd lose them. By the time I returned to base, I was a wreck."

"Did you cry?" I asked, unable to keep the hope from my voice. Not that I wanted him to have cried. I just didn't want to be the only one.

"Worse." His smile became wry as he traced his thumb over the seam of my lips. "I passed out in front of my boss."

I laughed at the image of this big, strong guy going down.

He softly traced a fingertip under my eyes, following the line of the bruises. "My teammates teased me for months."

How I loved the feel of his hands on me. And as I stood there, my amusement with him faded, opening a wide cataclysm of awareness. I stared at him, needing something. Another kiss?

His humor faded, too, like he'd read my thoughts. His entire body stiffened. "I'm going to kiss you," he said roughly.

I licked my lips in welcome invitation. "Yes."

His brown eyes heated and heated and heated. "I shouldn't. You're too young for me."

"I'm eighteen. An adult."

"The things I've seen, the things I've done, the things I *will* do. I shouldn't do this." But he meshed his lips to mine, his tongue thrusting past my teeth and beginning a wild dance with mine. He tasted hot and minty, just as I remembered. I wrapped my uninjured arm around his waist, pulling him closer.

His head angled to the side as he claimed and conquered more of my mouth. Warmth spread to every corner of my body, invading warmth, drugging warmth. Better than this morning.

One of his hands traced the ridges of my spine and stopped at the curve of my butt. His other hand tangled in my hair.

On and on the kiss continued, so decadent. So wild and wonderfully wicked. I moaned in excitement.

But when his hand began to inch up my T-shirt, skin on skin, and my hand began to inch up his, skin on skin, he stilled. He fisted the material for several seconds, then tore his mouth from mine.

He was panting; I was panting.

"Sorry," he said harshly. He regarded me with longing—a look I'm sure I returned. "You're not ready for this."

"I am. Swear to God I am. I want to go further," I admitted. And I did, I realized. I was ready, so ready, to take that next step. I loved him. He was more than just Erik Troy to me. He was savior, he was friend. He was pure excitement, absolute bravery.

"I want to go further, too. So badly," he added, his gaze roving over me. "But I want you to be sure. Have you ever . . . ?"

I blushed. "No."

"That's not something to be embarrassed about. That's something to be proud of." He leaned down and placed a soft kiss on my still-tingling lips, lingering, breathing me in as I breathed him in.

"Have you?" I asked, even though I knew the answer.

There was a pause. Then, "Yeah. For years, Cara was the only girl I'd been with. After we split, well, I'm ashamed to say I went a little crazy and slept with any girl who would have me. I stopped completely when I signed up at the high school."

Other boys would not have stopped, I suspected.

"I don't want to die without ever doing it," I told him. "But I don't want to be with anyone but you."

Erik stepped forward, closer to me, forcing me to back up.

"What—where?" My knees hit the edge of something and I tumbled down, landing on soft cushions. The couch.

Erik eased on top of me, then shifted his weight so that our sides pressed together.

He kissed me once, twice, sweet kisses, innocent kisses, and then he deepened the contact, brushing my lips apart with his tongue. I moaned into his mouth and he swallowed the sound, feeding me wanton tastes of passion.

"I could kiss you for hours," he said.

"Prove it," I replied, and he chuckled softly.

Our tongues twined and sparred and danced and caressed. For the longest time, he didn't do anything with his hands except hold me. But as *my* hands roamed underneath his T-shirt, over the hot skin of his back, he was spurred into action. His fingertips trekked along my stomach, swirled in my belly button, and I trembled.

"Feels good," I breathed.

"Feels amazing." He inched those naughty fingers higher, until he reached my breast. I wasn't wearing a bra. When he cupped, kneaded, pinched my nipple, I cried out. "Want me to stop?"

"No. No stopping."

"More?" Even as he spoke, he once again teased and taunted my nipple.

"More," I said on a groan.

He rolled slightly, placing himself between my legs. His lower half arched forward, back, forward, rubbing between my legs. I gasped at the dizzying contact and even met him halfway, needing that hard press.

He hissed out a breath. His movements became more frantic, more forceful.

Something was building inside me. A pressure. A need. A fog. All three blended together, consuming me. My mind focused on Erik, on his hands, on his body. I wanted our clothes off, didn't want a barrier between us.

"More," I said.

He lowered his arm and dabbled at the waist of my sweatpants. I tensed in anticipation of what he'd do next. *Dip lower. Touch me* where I ached. Please. Even as I thought it the plea burst from my lips. "Please."

Air caught in my throat as Erik did indeed sink his hand lower. Lower still. And then his fingers were where I'd wanted them, touching, moving in a way that lanced sensation after sensation through me. My legs fell farther apart. I clutched his shoulders, undulating against him. Moaning, almost sobbing.

You should be embarrassed. You sound ridiculous. I pressed my lips together, trying to cut off the noises I was making. I just . . . I felt so good. So close to something good and right and magnificent.

"Let me hear you," he said. "I want to hear that you like it."

Another moan pushed its way from me, so intense I *couldn't* hold it back. His words and his actions combined to destroy all my inhibitions, leaving only reaction. "Erik," I panted.

"You're almost there. So close."

His voice sounded strained. I forced my eyes open—when had I closed them?—and saw that his face was tense. Sweat beaded his forehead. Lines bracketed his eyes. But there was such heat, such need, such bliss in his eyes as he stared down at me, watching me. Then he moved his fingers expertly, a simple twist, but it was enough. Stars exploded in my mind. I shouted, spasmed, shouted some more. Always his name, though. Always his name.

He held me through it all, stroking me, telling me how beautiful I was. Long moments passed before I was calm enough to melt against him. My heart had yet to slow down.

"I have to get up now," he said. His voice was strained.

"What? No." I shook my head, locking my arms around him to hold him in place. I never wanted to let him go.

"Yes. Must."

"Why?" I asked, trying not to show my disappointment. We hadn't had sex. I wanted to go all the way. I wanted more. Wanted all of him.

"The longer I hold you, the harder," he stopped himself and laughed wryly. "The more difficult it's going to be to move away without actually loving you."

I kissed his neck, licking the salty taste of him. "Then love me, I want you to."

A tremor moved through him and vibrated into me. "Earlier I promised you that I'd make you feel good, and I have. I don't want your first time to be while you're on the run."

"But—what about you? I want to make you feel good, too." If he'd teach me how . . . I'd be an expert student and willing to do extra credit.

He shook his head. "We'll wait until we're no longer in danger and make sure your first time is special."

Pouting, I bit my bottom lip. "That makes me want the danger over with now."

"Me, too," he said. He swooped in for another kiss before rising from the couch. "Me, too."

I knew that boys often used girls sexually, then pretended not to know them. Or worse, made fun of them and called them names afterward. I'd seen it happen to many girls at school. But I didn't think Erik would be that way. He was just so different from every other boy I'd ever known. And the fact that he wanted my first time to be special, well, I fell a little more in love with him in that moment.

Who was I kidding? I'd fallen completely in love with him yesterday, when he'd done everything in his power to protect me.

My determination to survive this ordeal doubled. Tripled. I'd do whatever it took to win and be with Erik. Jump through fire—no problem. Hailstorms, acid rain, gunfire, flood—bring it on.

I should have known that thought would get me in trouble. Big trouble.

12

While we waited for night to fall—and to keep our minds off sex—Erik taught me how to defend myself. He taught me the best way to make and use a fist. The best places to kick an agent to topple him. Not in the groin, as I'd supposed, but in the trachea or vital organs: lungs, stomach, heart, kidneys.

"It'll bring them down every time," he'd instructed, "and it will keep them down, the most important factor. Because once you've engaged in battle and rendered pain, they'll forget about questioning you, forget about taking you in alive, and go for the kill. You want them on the ground as quickly as possible, unable to get up."

Scary stuff. But I loved it.

Best of all, he taught me how to fight while protecting my injured arm. I had to keep that side of my body angled *toward* my opponent and lash out with the other side, forcing them to try and stop *that* side of me.

Again, it was scary to think about doing any actual fighting, but I was happy to learn, to prepare, just in case.

Finally, though, darkness arrived and our reprieve was over.

Erik checked the monitors to make sure there were no agents in the area. There weren't. He even called Silver and made sure all was well. Thankfully it was. Silver and Shanel were back at Silver's house, surrounded by his father's guards. They'd led A.I.R. around the city most of the day, keeping several agents away from *us*.

Still, I was nervous as we stepped outside. Cool air kissed me, no longer warm and heavy. Golden moonlight drenched the night, illuminating the surrounding buildings, the humans and Outers striding down the sidewalks, the cars speeding along the streets.

Erik maintained a steady hold on my hand and we did our best to appear like an everyday, average couple just out for a nighttime stroll. To be honest, I felt exposed, as if everyone was staring at me, marking me for death.

"Maybe I shouldn't have colored my hair so *blue*," I said nervously.

"You look cute."

I grinned and squeezed his hand.

"You're hiding in plain sight, so no worries. You'll see."

At least I wasn't the only one hiding in plain sight. His

hair was bleached white with streaks of vivid red. He'd even painted a cobra tattoo on his neck. The snake's body stretched up to his left cheek and wrapped around his ear. Magnetic piercings dotted his eyebrow and lip. "Maybe we're a little too plainly in 'sight.'"

"No such thing." He leaned down and kissed my ear.

A shiver stole through me.

To go with our new hair, we also wore new clothes. He'd had a stash of different types and sizes at the safe house. Erik had chosen a black syn-leather duster and pants, which complimented the hard planes of his body.

He looked like an agent.

I wore a blood-red dress and spiked collar. Thigh-high boots hugged my legs and hid several blades. Erik had wanted me to be prepared for anything.

"See," he muttered, drawing my attention to his mouth. "No one wants to look at us. In fact, they're doing everything they can to *avoid* looking at us."

I studied people's faces as we passed them. Sure enough, they spied us and quickly glanced away, like we were visual poison. Plus, Outers gave Erik a wide birth, as if they feared he would arrest them.

I began to relax. We were making our way to some warehouse to get the supply of Onadyn he needed. Then we were going to distribute it to the aliens he'd promised it to. Aliens who might be dying, even now.

He'd told me the plan and had given me a chance to stay

behind. I hadn't taken it. No longer could I ignore the fact that innocent people were dying.

We walked several miles. An eternity. No more stealing cars for us. If it was called in, A.I.R. would know what vehicle to look for and we'd be caught before we could snap our fingers. We also got on and off different buses, sometimes just going in circles to make sure we weren't being followed.

During our travels, the poor part of the city gave way to the middle class, and by the time we exited our last bus, we were in the Northern District, the wealthy part of town. Here, the houses seemed to stretch to the sky. All of them were white and chrome, probably had the latest robotic security systems.

"The lab is here? In this neighborhood?" I asked, incredulous.

"Yep."

"But this place is . . ." I didn't know how to finish that sentence.

"Perfect for an illegal lab," Erik said. "Law enforcement, even A.I.R., usually give wealthy humans preferential treatment. They don't bust into these houses without proper paperwork, which takes time to acquire. Time for certain underpaid individuals to alert the homeowner. How do you think Silver's dad has survived so long in the business?"

"Ahhh."

"Onadyn and the equipment to make it can be removed from the dwelling in minutes, leaving the agents empty-handed when they're finally allowed to invade. Happened to me many times when I worked for A.I.R. I'd know beyond any doubt that drugs were inside a home, but by the time I got my warrant, the owner had cleaned the place out."

Remaining in the shadows, we edged to the side of one particular house. A robodog barked in the background. A wide iron fence stretched from the center of each side and angled backward, blocking in the grounds. Two towering white columns opened to a bricked pathway, which was lined with fake trees and led to an arched entrance.

Welcome, the place seemed to say. *Nothing bad happens here. Nothing illegal.*

Silver had given Erik the security code before we'd left the safe house. Thankfully Onadyn operations had been shut down temporarily due to A.I.R. interest, so we didn't have to worry about stumbling upon other employees while we "worked."

I'm now a thief, I thought.

The closer we came to the front door, the brighter the motion light shined, pushing away the comforting shadows. That didn't slow us down as we trekked up the steps.

"Stay here," Erik said, depositing me on a swinging bench and striding to the French double doors. He punched a series of numbers into the ID box and the entrance opened eagerly, like it had been waiting for him all day. He disappeared inside.

I was alone.

Several minutes passed. Long minutes. Torturous minutes.

What was going on in there? The robodog barked again and I gulped. A part of me feared A.I.R. agents would jump out at any second. "Erik!" I whispered fiercely.

Nothing.

"Erik!"

With a shaky hand, I withdrew a knife from my boot. The hilt was cool and heavy. Menacing. At least the neighborhood was calm and—

Headlights appeared in the distance. I shot to my feet and raced inside the house. I closed the door behind me and pressed my back against the frame, trying unsuccessfully to control my shallow breathing. My heartbeat galloped at full speed. Logically I knew A.I.R. would not announce their presence with blaring headlights. (Or would they?) They would have sneaked up on me so that I couldn't warn Erik. (Right?)

Oh God. I didn't know.

I turned and surveyed the house. The foyer was empty, devoid of furniture. Total silence. "Erik!" I hissed.

My voice echoed.

Where was he?

I held the knife in front of me and inched forward. Had he left the house? No, he wouldn't have abandoned me. Right? Right. Was he hurt? Knocked out? Totally fine and simply going about his plan without any thought to the fact that I might want to throw up?

Or, what if there *were* people here and he'd been subdued?

Total panic filled me. Paranoia. Terror. I forced my back to straighten and my shoulders to square. *All right. Here's what you're going to do, Robins. You're going to search the house and incapacitate anything that moves.* Yes. That's what I'd do.

"I was just coming to get you," a sweet, familiar voice said.

I gasped, my wild gaze searching the darkness. Erik stood beside me but I hadn't heard or seen his approach. Scowling, I slapped his shoulder. "I was just about to do a search and rescue. You have no idea how close you came to feeling the sting of my knife."

To his credit, he didn't laugh.

I slapped his shoulder a second time. "I was worried about you. You didn't tell me how long you'd be gone before you entered the house. You didn't tell me what to do if I spotted anyone."

He confiscated the knife and slid it back into my boot. I think I saw the hint of a smile. "On edge, are we?"

"I saw a car," I told him.

"Camille, sweetie, people do drive through neighbor-hoods."

Sweetie. I rubbed my hands up and down my forearms. "Why'd you leave me out there anyway?" I grumbled.

His hand tangled in my hair, pulling me forward for a quick kiss. "I wanted to make sure the house was safe first."

Hmm, I forgot everything but Erik when he kissed me like that. "And is it?"

He nodded. "It's just you and me, babe."

"Did you find the the stuff?"

The mention of Onadyn caused his eyes to go a little flat. "Yeah. But I want you to wait here while I gather it up."

No way. "I'll help."

"Nope." He shook his head, several white strands of hair falling over his forehead. "You're already involved in this mess, so there's nothing I can do about that, but I *can* make sure you don't actually handle the goods."

I anchored my hands on my hips and stared up at him. He wasn't doing this without me, wasn't taking the responsibility and the blame for his own. I *was* involved now; he was right about that. And I *would* be doing my part; he was so wrong about me not handling the goods. "I'm going to help."

"Nope," he repeated. "Sorry."

My eyes narrowed to tiny slits. He hated that he had to break the law, I realized that. And he didn't want me to have to hate it, as well. The more time I spent with Erik, the more I peeled away his layers and discovered the honorable guy underneath. But I wasn't going to let him do this alone.

"I want to help the Outers, Erik, and I'm willing to break the law to do it. Let me help. Please. Let me make a difference. What we're doing isn't something we should be ashamed of. This *needs* to be done."

A pause. Heavy, unsure. Wistful.

Then the flatness of his dark eyes began to give way to light, a shining gold. "I don't think I've ever met a girl like

191

you, Camille." He kissed me again, lingering this time. Savoring.

"I've ignored aliens most of my life, not helping when they were teased and taunted. I think it's time I crawled out from under my rock and saw the world for what it really is: a sometimes violent place in need of change and more people willing to step out and do something good, something right." *And maybe one day*, I thought, *I'll be able to do even more.* Maybe I'd be able to actually change the law.

Hopefully my dad had already started . . .

Hope rushed through me. By now, my mom had to have told him what I'd said. My dad had to have paid attention and was now doing everything in his power for the cause.

The cause. My cause. *Our* cause. Tolerance. Acceptance of differences.

"Time is our enemy, I'm assuming," I said, all business, "so show me where that Onadyn is."

Without any more hesitation, Erik ushered me out of the foyer and into a room at the top of the staircase. No, not a room. A laboratory. The air smelled sterile, layered with chemicals. Throughout the entire enclosure, there were long tables, each loaded down with decanters and pots. Lab coats hung on the hooks beside the door, as well as boxes of gloves. There was even a stove—or what looked to be a stove with four fire rings.

"It's amazing, really," Erik said. "The stuff in here can kill humans in the blink of an eye but it can save certain Outers just as quickly. Be careful. Don't touch anything that has liquid inside." He moved forward, but paused midstep. "I don't want you to suffocate."

Me either.

"It's an ugly death. The skin turns blue, flaky, and sinks in. The eyes bug out. Limbs flail as the body fights for a single drop of breathable air."

Images played through my mind and I cringed at the horror of it.

"Most humans have accepted our visitors. But there are still those who fear them. I understand that fear, I really do, because some aliens can walk through walls or simply disappear. Some can control our actions with their minds. But like humans, there are good and bad."

I'm guilty of that fear myself, I thought, a little sadly. *Never again,* I vowed.

Erik raked a hand through his hair. "I was never allowed here, though I fought and fought to gain an invitation. Funny that it took an A.I.R. arrest to get me in." He gave me another of those swift kisses. For strength? It was almost as if he couldn't stop himself, as if he *had* to kiss me. Was compelled by a force greater than himself to do it.

I hoped he would never stop.

"Look around. I'm going to check the Onadyn and make sure the vials are sealed properly before you touch them."

"Okay."

He strode to a cabinet in back, opened the doors by cutting the ID wires and rehooking them. ID boxes were supposedly thief proof, but I'd seen him bypass many with ease.

I walked to the closest table and lifted one of the empty decanters. There was a blue crust on the rim. Careful not to actually touch it, I sniffed. There was a subtle hint of . . . jasmine? Orchid? Some type of flower, definitely.

"Have you ever tried Onadyn?" I asked, setting the bottle down.

"No," Erik said. "Never."

"Ever thought about it?"

Several seconds ticked by in silence. I glanced over at him. He had his back to me and was rummaging through a metal box. "Yeah," he finally said. "Once or twice after I was kicked out of A.I.R. and faced a lifetime of imprisonment. I wasn't sure I could go on. I wasn't sure I *wanted* to go on."

I lifted another glass, one with pink striations on the bottom. Glitter seemed to cake the inside of it, like a snow globe. "What stopped you?"

He shrugged. "Thoughts of death. Addiction. Most of all, thoughts of becoming sloppy and forgetting who I am, caring only about my next high."

Before I could reply, a board creaked. The sound scared me and I froze, heart hammering. Erik didn't seem to notice or mind, so I forced myself to relax. "I don't understand why we're stealing from Silver's dad. We could have asked him and saved ourselves the trouble of breaking in."

"He never would have given us what we needed and now

that A.I.R.'s found me, I'm sure they've frozen my accounts. I wouldn't have been able to buy it."

"But I thought Silver's dad was sympathetic to the cause."

"He is, but only for his family. Everyone else has to pay. He's gotten used to his lifestyle, I guess."

I pushed out a sigh. "Silver's cheating his dad, then. Can we trust him not to change his mind and tattle?"

"Yeah. It's, uh, not the first time he's had to go to such lengths." A pause, then a happy *whoop*. "Found it!" He pocketed several small vials of clear liquid. I'd never done Onadyn, either, and didn't ever want to—for all the reasons he'd named.

"One day we might get a medal of honor for this," I told him. Did I believe it? No. But it was a nice thought.

He tossed me a grin, the expression somehow sad.

"Well, it's possible," I said, refusing to back down.

Several more vials found their way into his pockets. "So is this the wildest thing you've ever done?" he asked, changing the subject.

"Yes. No question. You?"

"Nah. Going back to high school tops the list for me. Those first few days, I was convinced someone was going to realize I wasn't who I said I was and I didn't belong there."

Approaching him, I traced a fingertip over the tabletop. "But no one did."

"Sometimes people only see what they want to see." He paused a moment to look over at me.

"I certainly did." Grinning, I closed the rest of the distance until I stood beside him. "Since you're stuffing them in your pockets, I'm going to assume the vials are sealed properly."

"They are, but I still don't want you to handle them." He closed the cabinet with a soft *click*, then turned toward me. "Ready?"

Clearly he still wanted to carry the bulk of the responsibility on his own shoulders. I, however, was having none of that.

"Nope," I said. "Not quite yet." Rising on my tiptoes, I planted a kiss on Erik's welcoming lips, just as he'd done to me several times. But I didn't embrace him. I jabbed a hand into his pocket and withdrew a fistful of the vials. I shoved them in my pockets, peering up at him and silently daring him to say something. "Now I'm ready. You're not doing this alone."

He shook his head, but admiration glowed in his eyes. "You constantly amaze me," he said, not trying to take them away.

"Thank you," I said primly.

"You're very welcome," he said, mimicking my tone.

We shared a laugh.

We left the lab then and descended the staircase. I could hear the vials clanging together every time Erik moved. My dress was so tight the vials had no wiggle room and remained in place.

"I can't believe I'm doing this," I said when we reached the front entrance. "Where are the Outers staying anyway? The ones who need the Onadyn?"

"Southern District on Main. The Offworlder Apartments, which should have collapsed years ago. I'm sorry, but we've got a long hike ahead of us."

"I'll live."

He pried the double doors apart, rather than mess with the ID box and code again. "You're—"

"Caught," a woman said just in front of us. It was Phoenix. Wisps of brown hair whipped around her smug features. She aimed a pyre-gun at Erik's chest. "You're caught."

13

In the ensuing seconds that seemed to take an eternity to tick by, chaos erupted. Erik had *his* gun aimed at Phoenix before I could draw in a panicked breath. Other A.I.R. agents surrounded us, a thousand it seemed, weapons poised and ready to fire.

Death had never seemed closer.

"We can't thank you enough for showing us the lab's location," Cara said, stepping forward until she stood beside Phoenix. She appeared just as smug as her coworker.

I grit my teeth.

"You didn't follow us here," Erik said stiffly. He held the gun steady, seemingly unimpressed by the agents and the weapons they'd trained on him. "How did you find us?"

There was a man standing on Phoenix's other side and he laughed, drawing attention to himself. "I just got into town, haven't been briefed because I've been too busy fighting Morevvs, but even I can tell you the answer to that."

"Ryan," Erik said, shoulders tensing. The name was spat out, as if it was the darkest curse. He inched forward, scooting me behind him as best he could so that I was out of the line of fire.

Ryan was obviously a few years older than Erik. He had dark hair and eyes so blue they sparkled. He was handsome and muscled and wore all black. And he was grinning like it was Christmas and he'd gotten exactly what he wanted from Santa. "If I know my girl, she pegged you with a GPS chip."

Erik growled low in his throat.

"Yep. That's exactly what I did." As unconcerned as Erik had first seemed, Phoenix unsheathed a blade and reached around him. She stabbed the silver tip into one of the welts on his upper back.

He didn't move, didn't show any reaction, though it had to have hurt.

When she pulled away, there was blood on her hand and on the knife and a tiny black dot on the tip of her index finger. "That's why we whipped you. That, and you deserve a little punishment for what you've put us through. There was a sedative on the whip. You passed out and we were then able to inject the chip without your knowledge. And you never suspected, because you simply assumed your back hurt from the whipping."

"You—you—"

"Outsmarted you," Phoenix interjected.

My hands tightened into fists, but I forced myself to relax, to touch his back in comfort. He, too, relaxed.

"There'll be no escaping this time," Phoenix said, scowling. I guess she hadn't gotten the reaction she wanted. "And guess what? There'll be no help from your Morevv buddies, either. We've got them surrounded, too. And they're going to pay. They injured Bradley."

Shanel, I thought. Silver. No, no, no. Were they okay?

"Now, why don't you drop the gun," Ryan said, losing his smile. "I don't want to kill you, but we both know I'll do it in a heartbeat. You do *not* hold a gun on Phoenix. Ever."

Erik didn't drop his gun, but he did raise his free hand as if he meant to give up. I knew he had a knife strapped to his wrist, so the action would arm him further, not leave him vulnerable. Still. Defeat pressed heavily on my shoulders.

Defeat? *That's the old Camille.* The new-and-improved Camille did not give up, did not back down. I'd come too far to be captured now. *You have weapons, too. Remember? You aren't helpless.*

"You, too, Camille," Phoenix said, perhaps sensing what I meant to do next. "Hands up."

I didn't move. Not yet, not yet . . . *Oh God. Oh God. Can't believe you're doing this, can't believe you're even thinking it.*

Start believing, I thought, eyes narrowing as determination rushed through me, strengthening me.

"Dragging innocent girls down with you." Ryan *tsk*ed under

his tongue. "Sinking lower every day. Troy, is it? That the new last name you gave yourself? Funny. Troy was defeated, too."

"Like you have room to talk about dragging innocent girls into the gutter," Erik snarled. His finger twitched on the trigger. "You started dating Phoenix when she was your student. How depraved is that?"

Anger darkened Ryan's features, not hot enough to be classified as rage, but hot all the same. "Don't bring Phoenix into this."

"Don't bring Camille into it, either. She's done nothing wrong."

"Then why are Onadyn vials sticking out of her dress pockets?" Cara demanded, no longer content to remain in the background.

The agent named Kitten stepped into my line of vision, at the corner of my eye. I could see that she was programming her gun and aiming at Erik.

Act now, Robins. You won't have another opportunity.

Before I could talk myself out of it, I kicked up one leg and my boot banged into Phoenix's wrist. The action startled her and knocked the gun out of her hand. With barely a pause, I spun and grabbed hold of Erik.

Everything that followed seemed to happen in slow motion, but I knew—logically, at least—that everything was moving quickly. I jerked Erik past the front door. His reflexes were stellar and he knew exactly what I wanted him to do without being told. He slammed the door closed.

Pop. Whiz.
Pop. Whiz.
Sizzle. Sizzle.

Agents fired, some using pyre-fire, some using bullets. The bullets created gouges and the fire melted bits of the metal.

"Run, Camille," Erik shouted. I expected him to grab me and leap into a sprint. He didn't. He walked backward, his gun now trained on the door as he waited for A.I.R. to break through. A knife rested in his other hand, like I'd suspected.

For the first time, I noticed that there weren't any windows.

I remained in place. Behind me, I could hear footsteps and knew A.I.R. was closing in, blocking every possible avenue of escape. "They're everywhere! We have to leave." Panic rolled through me, thick and oppressive. Almost debilitating. Almost. "Now! Come on!"

"Damn it, Camille. Listen to me this time and run. Hide. If they take both of us, we're lost. The cause is lost; Outers will die."

"No."

"Houses like this are made to withstand attack, but it won't hold out much longer. You have to go. Now."

"I can't." I shook my head. "I can't leave you. I won't."

"Take the Onadyn and run, damn it." He didn't face me, but continued to face the door. Waiting . . . "I'm begging you! I've worked too hard for those kids to die now."

Run.

Stay. Don't be a coward. Help him!

No, you have to run. You have to save those kids.

Ohmygod, I couldn't decide. Didn't know what to do. I moved, stopped, moved, stopped. Unsure. So unsure. What a horrible decision to make—and not a lot of time to make it. Save the Outers or try and save Erik. If it were just me, I'd leave. Right now. No hesitation. But Erik . . .

"I'll stay and hold them off and *you* take the drugs." He'd do better at evading capture. And I, well, I'd survived A.I.R. once. I could do it again. And if I didn't, I will have gone down with a fight.

"Camille." My name was a curse, a prayer, an ache. "You know that won't work. They'll have you pinned in minutes and be after me immediately after. I can hold them off longer, giving you the needed time. Just go!"

"Erik. Please. I can't leave you," I whispered brokenly.

Growling low in his throat, he spun toward me and fired a shot at my feet. I jumped. Yellow beams sizzled at the ground where I'd stood. "Stop! What are you doing?"

"Go!"

Still I held firm. "You'll be able to hide better and—"

"They might kill you this time, Camille. Now do you understand? I'd rather the Outers die than you. Understand?" He fired another shot, this one closer. "Go! Help them and stay low."

"Erik."

"Go!" Another shot.

I jumped away from it, never taking my gaze from him. An eternity passed while I gazed into his dark eyes. A mere second.

"Go."

"Okay," I said. Tears burned my eyes as I inched backward. They were different than any I'd shed before. They weren't born of fear; they weren't born of upset. They were born of hope and desperation. "Okay." *You're leaving him? Coward!*

No, not a coward. I was giving up something I loved to save others. Leaving him was the right choice—not the best, not something I wanted. It was tearing me up inside, but it would save those aliens. Still, the tears flowed freely down my cheeks.

Just then, the front door burst open, as did several of the windows in the upstairs rooms. Erik tore his focus from me and fired at the agents who were even now pounding their way inside. No, he wasn't aiming at them, I realized, plastering myself against the wall, trembling, crying harder, because he didn't really want to hurt or kill them. He was aiming *toward* them, trying to keep them back and buy the promised time.

More footsteps echoed behind me.

Using the shadows to my advantage, I scrambled toward the back of the house. Agents seemed to be everywhere, like flies, buzzing in every direction. They were black slashes of lethal power. Menacing death wielders.

How was I going to get out of here undetected?

A few seconds later, several of the agents spotted me

and rushed for me. I remained in place, unsure what to do. Weapon . . . I had a weapon, right? I was just reaching into my boot, fingers curling around the hilt of a blade, when the first agent reached me. He backhanded me across the face and I cried out. I flew to the ground, knife forgotten, blood already trickling from my mouth.

Still in his line of sight, Erik witnessed the entire thing. He roared a loud, high-pitched, piercing animal sound. An amber beam erupted.

The guy who'd hit me fell to the ground beside me, a blackened hole sizzling in his chest. He didn't move. Dead. He was dead. I glanced up, wide-eyed, to see Erik's gun smoking. He'd killed him. For me. He hadn't killed for himself, but he'd killed for me.

He fired at the others as they surged forward, forgetting me in their haste to stop Erik. When they reached him, they jumped on him, knocking him down, hitting and kicking him.

"No," I screamed, shoving to my feet. *No!*

Boom!

An explosion rocked the entire house, throwing me onto my butt. Plumes of smoke wafted through the air, thicker than before. Rocks and timber rained. Erik, I suspected, had somehow created this distraction for me. I couldn't leave, though. Not until I knew he was okay.

I once again pushed to shaky legs and glanced around, my eyes burning and watering. My nostrils stung. People were lying on the ground, moaning. Other were silent, unconscious or dead.

"Erik?" I coughed. "Erik?"

No response.

"Erik!" Pure, undiluted panic filled me. I didn't see him. Where was he? My gaze landed outside, past the entrance that had been destroyed by the blast. I gasped, both relieved and horrified. Phoenix, Ryan, Cara, and Kitten had Erik pinned to the ground. But he was still fighting. With all of his strength, he was still fighting, his body bucking. His limbs flailing.

I wanted so badly to go to him. To help him. To do something, anything, to save him. He'd shown me some basics today, but I knew deep down such moves would never defeat these people. If I tried, I'd be captured, too. I knew it. He knew it, that's why he'd told me to run. There was no denying it, no fooling myself. These agents were highly trained and by their sheer number they soon managed to subdue Erik completely.

I couldn't help him and help the Outers who needed the Onadyn I carried.

Once again I was faced with a choice. I'd thought I'd made it, thought I was prepared to run, but seeing Erik so helpless . . .

I could let the aliens die or try and free Erik with no guarantee that I'd succeed, perhaps destroying this opportunity he'd given me. *Evade capture now and you can fight to get him released later.*

But I can't leave him behind. Not like this.

You have to. You have to remain free, so you can rescue him and Silver and Shanel. He knew this would happen.

Unsure, I bit my bottom lip.

Erik wants you to leave. Think of all he's done for you. Now you must do this for him.

That finally convinced me. More than anything, Erik wanted those Outers saved. He'd given up his life and his career for them. And now, I would give up my own desires for them. No, for him. For Erik.

Blinking back my tears, I spun on my heel and ran. Just ran.

━━━━━

When I hit a public street, I flagged down a cab. I told the driver to take me to the Southern District, and his mocha-colored face paled.

"Sure you want to go there?" he asked, his disgust clear.

I nodded. Sweat poured from me. Breath emerged shallow and quick. I constantly stole glances out the back window, expecting to see agents as we sped down the road. Thankfully, I didn't. A thousand times I rubbed the back of my neck, my shoulders making sure there was no welt there. If they'd implanted a GPS chip . . .

I tried not to think about that. I tried not to think of Erik, of what was happening to him. They wouldn't kill him.

They'd said as much. Or had they been lying in an attempt to make him cooperate? They had what they wanted now. The lab. The drugs.

Please keep Erik safe, I prayed.

We reached the Southern District twenty minutes later and I paid the driver with cash Erik had tucked into my boot earlier. *Just in case,* he'd said.

Shaking, I stepped outside, already scanning for the apartment building Erik had mentioned. The night air was still cool, but it did little to soothe the burn of my exhaustion and fear. The cab sped away, tires squealing.

I spotted the building just ahead, and my stomach bottomed out. The Offworlder Apartments.

Crumbling, just as Erik had said. There were holes in the sides and one half of the roof was missing. I tentatively approached. A naked, drunken Mec was sprawled in front of the steps, snoring in his sleep. He'd thrown up on his own legs and bits of it were dried on his white skin.

Cringing, I hopped over him. I searched my brain, but couldn't recall Erik giving me a specific apartment number. Damn this! If necessary, I'd knock on every door.

There was no one in the bottom-level rooms, so I took the steps to the second floor. Several of the steps were missing and others were simply broken slabs of concrete. Falling into a dark abyss was a very real possibility. Dirt and grime covered every inch of the place and the smell of urine, sweat, and rotting food permeated the air. The higher I stepped, the more I gagged.

I checked every single apartment on that floor, and then the third. I met some angry Outers who waved fists in my face and pushed me away from their doors. I even met a few humans who wanted to sell me their "services."

I was proud of myself. I didn't run away.

On the fourth floor, I encountered several different alien species, but all of them wore ragged clothing and looked thin as sticks. One brave soul, a male teenager protecting his territory, waved a knife at me. I showed him mine, which was bigger, and he backed away.

I didn't want to hurt him; I wanted to cry.

I'd never seen such poverty in my life and everything inside of me was crumbling as surely as the building. No one answered the door at the next apartment and the door was unlocked, so I tentatively pushed my way inside. Death hung in the air, thick, black. Gasping moans echoed in my ears. In that moment I knew, *knew,* this was it.

A pale-skinned Zi Kara lay on her stomach, a cup beside her, liquid still wetting the dirty shag carpet. It looked like she'd been walking from the kitchen and simply collapsed. Her head was tilted to the side and I could see that her eyes were open, glassy, and fixed straight ahead.

Zi Karas were long and lean, with smooth gray skin, almost like that of a seal. Right now her skin appeared tinted yellow. *Please be alive,* I prayed.

Crouching down beside her, I gently rolled her over. Her lips were tinted yellow, too, and raspy pants, shallow and light, escaped. She was alive! Slowly her black eyes moved to me, beseeching, silently begging for help. Her cheeks, which should have been rounded, almost fat, were sunken in.

"Erik sent me," I said, grasping her under the neck and lifting. My heart broke for her. So helpless. So near death. *This didn't have to happen.* This should *not* have happened.

She opened her mouth to say something but no sound emerged.

I dug in my pocket and withdrew a vial. I popped the cork with my teeth, and a little of the liquid splashed on my tongue. Tasteless, I mused, a rush of dizziness hitting me. For a split second, my lungs froze, refusing to fill with air.

Panic didn't have time to take root. A second later, I was breathing normally. Dear Lord. Was that what addicts experienced? How could they stand it?

Shaking my head to regain focus, I poured the contents down the woman's throat. She swallowed greedily. At first, nothing happened. But slowly, so slowly, the yellow tint of her skin gave way to gray. Her glassy eyes cleared, making them appear like polished onyx.

"Children," she gasped, her voice heavily accented. "My children."

I pushed to my feet and hurried through the apartment. One child, a little boy, was sprawled out on the bathroom floor. The other, a teenage girl, was propped on her bed, staring out at the world silently.

I fed them both a vial of Onadyn.

They were slower to recover than their mother. And for a long while I didn't think the boy would make it. Even with the drug, he was weak and helpless. More tears burned my eyelids.

No wonder Erik fought so hard for these people.

This was terrible. So terrible. So cruel.

These aliens were innocent. How could A.I.R. deny them Onadyn like this? How?

A family like this should not be punished for another's sins. Innocent. *Innocent.* The word continually echoed through my mind. For so many years I'd been oblivious to this. Maybe I hadn't known because I hadn't wanted to know. Maybe the information simply wasn't accessible to the average citizen.

That didn't matter anymore.

Something had to be done.

I stayed at the apartment for over two hours, making sure the family was going to be okay. I let the mother—her name was Norenne—have all the vials. She carried four to her neighbor, who was in as bad shape as she had been.

The neighbor's children never woke up, though.

When I left, I was brokenhearted, torn up, but more determined than I'd ever been in my life. I was going to save Erik and I was going to save these Outers. Shy away from conflict? Never again!

14

After I'd purchased a disposable holocamera and taken pictures of the—I gulped, remembering—Outer's dead children, surely the most difficult thing I'd ever done, I walked to a payphone and dialed Shanel's number. I expected to leave a message, but she answered on the fourth ring.

"Yeah?" she asked, her voice raspy with . . . tears? Sleep?

"God, I'm so glad you're home," I breathed with relief. There was a street nearby and I wanted to jump out of my skin every time I saw a car. A few homeless stumbled along the sidewalk to my left. "Are you okay? Did they hurt you?"

"Camille? Is that you?"

"It's me."

"Sweet Jesus, I can't tell you how happy I am to hear your voice. Things were going so great, you know, and then they caught us! They surprised us, and I didn't know what to do. But you have to hang up," she said urgently. "I think they're tracking my calls. I think that's the only reason they released me. I mean, I'm okay. I'm in trouble with my dad, but they—" She choked on a sob. "They have Silver locked up. They questioned me and then sent me home."

"I'm glad you're okay," I told her. "I love you."

"You, too."

I disconnected. Shanel was safe, so that was one less worry. I only prayed A.I.R. *hadn't* traced my call. Just in case, I walked around the corner and used a different payphone to call my parents.

"Meet me in front of the Ship as soon as possible," I told them and hung up. I wanted to linger, talk to them, but couldn't risk it. Quaking, I hitched a ride on the bus. Every unexpected noise, every person that looked at me, nearly sent me into a whirlwind of panic.

Once there, I waited in the shadows, pressed up against the building. My heart nearly skipped a beat when I saw my parents' car. They pulled into the parking lot. I looked around, searching for any type of tail.

They didn't have one. That I could see. *You really going to do this?*

Oh yeah. Sweating, trying to stay in the shadows, I inched toward their car. They were parked and about to get out. I rushed forward, opened the back door, and threw myself inside, staying as low as possible. I'd stuffed the camera in my pocket and it scratched at my stomach.

Seeing me, both of my parents gasped.

"Drive, Daddy."

"Wh—"

"Drive!"

He gunned out of the parking lot, tires squealing.

My mom twisted and gazed down at me. "Camille, I don't even know what to say to you." Fright and relief infused my mother's voice.

"Don't look at me. Face forward. And watch for a tail."

She obeyed, crying, "Oh, baby. Oh, baby, baby, baby. I've been so worried."

I wanted so badly to hug her, but knew I couldn't. My gaze flicked to my dad. Even from his profile, I could see that his expression was stern and angry. His hair looked a little grayer and his face a little more lined.

"Young lady," were the first words out of his mouth. "You have a lot of explaining to do. Why is your hair blue? Why are you dressed like *that*? What's going on? I've never had to worry about you before and suddenly that's all I can do. A.I.R.? Onadyn?"

My mom reached back and grabbed on to my hand, squeezing. With her free hand, she wiped at the tears streaming down her cheeks. Her face was red and splotchy from crying. Her shirt was wrinkled at the side, as if she'd fisted the material one too many times.

Stay strong. "Have you looked into the Onadyn laws?" I asked. My legs were so weak I would have fallen if I'd been standing.

"No. There's no need. We're not getting involved."

"I have pictures," I said, reaching for the thin camera tucked in my pocket. "These Zi Karas are related to an Outer who committed a crime. They can't get the supply of Onadyn they need. They're dying. They're—"

"Destroy the pictures," my dad growled before I explained further. "We can't have any evidence linking you to other-worlder criminals."

"Daddy. Please. Just look." I held the camera up and out, pressing the button that caused one of the photos to crystallize, becoming a hologram.

Without taking his gaze from the road, he shook his head. "I don't want to see them. You are to do and say nothing that will incriminate you in any way."

Defeat seemed to be closing in around me, but I pressed on. "Aliens died, Daddy. I tried to save them by taking them Onadyn. I broke the law. Does that make me a bad person in your eyes? A criminal deserving of prison?"

His hard features crumbled, which almost made *me* crumble. "I thought I taught you better than this," he whispered brokenly. "I thought I taught you to put your own family first. Maybe I was a terrible parent. Maybe—"

"You're a wonderful parent," I said, cutting him off, "and I love you. But I've had my eyes opened. I can't pretend people aren't suffering. I can't pretend there's nothing I can do to help."

"I don't want to hear this. You're my only daughter. I want you safe. Always."

"Just hear me out. Please." When he remained silent, I let the story pour from me. Every detail. I left nothing out this time. As I spoke, they paled. They cried.

"Oh, Camille." My mom dropped her head into her waiting hands. "This might very well have earned you a life sentence."

I shoved the camera at them again, flicking through the bleak pictures one by one. "They're dying," I said. "Kids are dying because they can't get the Onadyn they need."

My dad scrubbed a hand down his face, and the action reminded me of Erik. *Erik.* Thinking of him caused my stomach to clench. What was A.I.R. doing to him?

Was he okay?

"I can't let you get any more involved in this, Camille," my dad said with a shake of his head. He wasn't angry now, he was sad. "You could be killed. You've already put your own life at risk. And your future—" He pressed his lips together and shook his head. "No. Sorry."

I peered up at him, my gaze unflinching. "I saved lives tonight. I made a difference. Together we can do more."

He waved a hand through the air, the action clipped, angry. "I don't care about the Outers. I care about you."

My mom's voice trembled when she said, "I can't lose you, baby. You're all I've got."

"You won't lose me," I promised, but we both knew that wasn't a promise I could realistically make. "If I survived tonight, I can survive anything."

"No," she said.

"No," my dad reiterated. "Do you know what would happen to me if I tried to change the Onadyn laws? I'd be fired. No other firm would hire me. We'd lose my income, and we'd lose our home, our cars, our food." His features hardened. "We'll take you to A.I.R. headquarters and tell them you were forced. They'll stop hunting you and we can pretend this night never happened."

Erik had given up everything for these people and my dad wanted to make it worse for him by saying he forced me. No damn way. I had to do something! Find someone who could help me. But who?

"You're bleeding," my mom suddenly gasped out.

I looked down at the bandage covering my upper arm. Tiny drops of blood had dried on the edges. I recalled how that woman, Mia, had squeezed the injury, trying to hurt me so that I'd tell her what she wanted to know. My eyes widened as an idea took root in my mind.

Mia had been hard; she'd been mean. But she'd been seeking the truth. Erik thought she was half-human, half-alien. If she was, she might understand. She might sympathize.

Would she help me, though? She thought I was guilty of selling drugs to humans. *You don't have anyone else right now.*

It was worth a shot.

The most Mia could do was kill me and that had been threatened so much it no longer bothered me. Which was as sad as it was empowering.

"You're taking me to A.I.R.?" I asked my dad.

"Yes. And I don't want you to talk to them. I'll handle everything. I'll do whatever it takes to clear your name."

I didn't contradict him. In fact, I sat up in the seat and waited.

15

Head high, I strolled into A.I.R. with my parents at my sides. The glass doors swished behind us and I studied my surroundings with trepidation. *It's not too late. You can still run.* I kept walking forward. Agents littered the lobby area, some striding back and forth with folders, others dragging screaming aliens to . . . God knows where. The cells?

I'd probably find out firsthand.

As we approached the front desk, I kept my shoulders squared and my features blank (I hoped). Of course, I was stopped before I reached my destination.

A computerized voice announced my entrance and sirens exploded into action.

"Now just a minute," my dad shouted. "She's innocent."

The male agent at the desk withdrew his pyre-gun and

aimed it at my heart. He scowled at me. "Stop! Stay right where you are. Hands up."

I obeyed without protest. "I'm unarmed," I told him, refusing to show fear. I'd left my knives in the car.

"She's unarmed," my dad shouted. "Put your weapon away."

My mom jumped in front of me, but I pushed her out of the way. Seconds later, a group of agents rushed me. They tackled me to the ground, knocking the air out of my lungs. Dazed, I didn't say a word as they banded my wrists and jerked me to my feet.

"Leave her alone," my dad snapped. "We're here to clear her name."

"Stay here, old man," one of the agents commanded.

They could have killed me and I half expected them to, but they didn't. Instead, they hauled me off while my dad yelled and my mom cried. I was escorted to a cell and strapped into a chair, just like before. Most of the debris from earlier had been cleaned away.

"I'd like to speak with Mia," I said, as confidently as I could. "I have information she wants."

He snorted and the group filed out of the room, leaving me alone.

How much timed passed, I didn't know. Every few hours, I was released from the chair and taken to a bathroom where a female guard watched me use the facilities. I'd never been so embarrassed in my life.

At one point, someone cleaned my wound and rebandaged

it. But finally, blessedly, Mia entered the cell. Not so blessedly, Phoenix and Cara were with her. All three women wore expressions of fury. And—dare I think—grudging respect?

"You have some information for me," Mia said. She stopped directly in front of me.

Eyeing her, I lifted my chin and fired off all the questions that had been building inside me. "How are my parents? Where's Erik? Is he okay?"

"You don't get to ask questions," Cara snapped. "You're as bad as he is, and you deserve the same punishment."

"You said you were innocent in all of this," Mia said to me.

"That was before." I lifted my chin another notch. *Don't back down.*

Cara arched a dark brow. "Before what? Before you started sleeping with Erik?"

If my hands had been free, I might have slapped her.

"Cara," Mia said. "If I have to send you from a cell one more time, you'll be riding a desk for the next month."

Cara pressed her lips together.

Mia nodded at me, a command to continue. "Tell me what you came to tell me."

"Erik hasn't been selling Onadyn to humans. He's been practically giving it away to Outers, for a fraction of the price he buys it for. He told me that he gave it to them without charge for a long time, but when he lost everything, he had to start selling. I—" *Come on, finish this!* "—took pictures of them to show how they die, how they suffer."

Mia's eyes narrowed, hiding the ice blue of her irises and leaving only black. "Where are the pictures now?"

"My dad has them. They might be in his car." If he'd destroyed them in an effect to protect me . . . I didn't know what I'd do. "Innocent aliens are dying, and *they* are who Erik wants to save. They're who *I* want to save."

"Doesn't matter," Mia said, showing no mercy. "Both of you broke the law."

I stared over at her, a thought sliding into place. "I noticed that one of your own agents, your own friend, is an alien. A Teran, I think. I saw her that first night, after the car chase, and a few times after."

"That's Kitten." Phoenix stepped toward me and she radiated an air of challenge.

"What if she was the one who needed it? What if she couldn't get it? You'd do anything to help her, right?" Helpless as I was, I forged ahead. "Erik has been helping a family survive, a family *he* loves. What crime is there in that?"

"You don't know what you're talking about," Cara said, but she'd lost the heat of her anger. She frowned down at me.

"Listen." Phoenix tilted her head to the side, studying me. "I was an addict," she confessed and the words surprised a gasp out of me. "I know what Onadyn can do to a person when it's abused. We regulate it to keep people from having to experience that. We regulate it to keep predatory aliens from staying here."

"A drug addict is going to be a drug addict, no matter how

many drugs you regulate," I pointed out. "And just because one alien in a family is predatory doesn't mean every other member is, too."

No one had a response to that.

"Get those pictures from my dad," I beseeched. "He might try and tell you that Erik forced me to help, but that's a lie. I didn't know what was going on last time we talked, but I do now. And I *am* helping Erik now. Willingly."

Absolute silence claimed the entire cell. My breath was ragged in my ears. Sweat beaded over me. So much hinged on what came next. So much.

Cara ran a hand down the length of her ponytail. "You could have doctored those photos. Looking at them won't change a damn thing."

I peered up at her again, fighting disappointment. "You dated Erik, so you know how kind and caring he is. How could you think, even for an instant, that he'd do this without a good reason? Or did you figure that out later and that's why you're so bitter?"

Before she could respond, I added, "How many times do I have to tell you this? He was protecting innocent lives. Isn't that what A.I.R. is supposed to do? Protect?"

"*Human* lives," Mia said, then frowned.

"Innocent lives," I repeated. If she *was* part alien, she had to see that. She had to accept it.

With a screech, Cara pulled out a gun and pointed it at me. Phoenix gaped at her. "Put the gun away, Cara. Now!"

I remained exactly as I was, not moving. My heart galloped in my chest. "Let her shoot me," I said bravely, uncaring. "I'm obviously an evil human. I've been, gasp, caught with drugs."

"Cara." Mia spoke low, quietly, but there was absolute command in her voice.

Cara's hand shook. "No. I will not lower my gun. I want her to admit she's done something wrong. Look at her, how smug and superior she is."

"You want me to admit I'm wrong? Why? So you can go on believing that you dumped Erik and turned your back on him for a good reason?" I laughed, but it was a scary sound. Not just devoid of humor like before but ragged, animalistic. "Deep down, you know you're the one who's wrong. Not me."

"Phoenix, go get Camille's dad and make sure he has those damn photos," Mia snapped.

Phoenix turned on her heel and strolled out without a word.

Cara kept the gun trained on me.

I began to sweat. Mia studied her nails, but I could feel the tension humming off her. Maybe my words were making her think. I could hope, at least.

An eternity later, Ryan and Phoenix strode into the cell. Their expressions were grim and their hands were empty.

"Where are they?" Mia demanded.

"Come with us," Ryan said. He worried two fingers over his mouth.

Mia's eyes narrowed, once again closing off the magnetic blue and leaving only those sharp, black pupils. "Why?"

"Erik is finally talking," Phoenix said. "He's ready to bargain."

"What?" Cara and I gasped in unison.

Mia uncuffed me from the chair and every single one of them left—even Cara and her gun—leaving me alone. Erik was bargaining? He'd vowed never to do that. Never to compromise. Worry poured through me as I massaged my wrists. Why would he do such a thing? Had they hurt him so horribly that he now had no other choice?

Damn it! I wanted answers and I wanted them now. "Show him to me on that screen," I shouted. But a minute ticked by, then another, and the screen never appeared.

I pushed to my feet and paced the length of the cell, cursing all the while. Was this my punishment? The torture of not knowing? Of wondering? *What are you telling them, Erik?* Finally, a few hours later, the entire gang returned. They looked tired, relieved, and angry all at once.

"What's going on?" I demanded. "What did he say?"

"You're free to go," Mia told me.

"What? Why? What's changed?"

Cara appeared at her side. She wouldn't meet my gaze; she looked just above my shoulder. "He bargained. For you." She spat the last word.

For me? In that moment, I didn't know what to think, what to feel or say.

"We have his full confession," Mia said. "He's going to help us infiltrate the ring."

"No." I stomped my foot. "No! People will die."

"No, because we're going to do all we can to help them."

My eyes widened and my heart slowed its erratic, angry beat. "Really?"

"Your dad gave us the pictures. That little girl . . ." Mia's voice trailed off. "What you and Erik did, well, it was wrong. The way you went about it was wrong. But the outcome was," she shrugged, "good. And it doesn't feel right to punish you for saving people from certain death." She paused, stared at me intently. "Your parents are here and they're eager to see you."

We'd won, I thought. We'd actually won! A small victory, but a victory all the same. I couldn't help myself; I whooped and hugged her. She didn't hug me back, but she did pat me on the shoulder. Her hair was as soft as my mother's, just as dark, and brushed my cheek.

"Onadyn won't be legalized anytime soon," she told me, "but you've brought it and the need for its correct distribution to our attention."

I couldn't stop grinning as she led me down a long, winding hall and into the A.I.R. lobby. My parents were seated on a couch and stood when they saw me. I rushed to my mom and she hugged me tightly, crying, "I'm so proud of you."

I pulled back and looked up at my dad. His features were stern. "I'm proud of you, too," he admitted. "What you did, well, you were right. I spoke out of worry for you before. Just don't ever scare me like that again, sweetheart. I love you too much to lose you."

He jerked me into his arms. I hugged him back with all my strength and didn't pull back until my injured arm screamed in protest.

"Camille?"

I heard Erik's voice and turned, gasping in delight when I saw him. He was cut up and bruised, more so than before, and dressed in a plain white prison uniform. His arm was in a sling, but he was alive. Joy washed through me, more joy than I'd ever known. I raced to him and threw myself into his arms.

He caught me and spun me around, one arm holding me up, kissing me deeply. "Are you okay?" he demanded a little while later, setting me down and cupping my jaw.

My dad cleared his throat. Erik and I separated reluctantly. I made the introductions.

"Just a minute more, Daddy," I said, not waiting for his reply as I pulled Erik into a shadowed corner.

"Are you okay?" Erik repeated when we were alone.

"I'm fine," I said. "What about you?" My gaze roved over his face, taking in every detail. "How are you? How do you feel?"

"Good, now that you're here. God, I missed you." He kissed me again, a quick meshing of lips that warmed me up.

When we pulled back, we stared at each other, grinning.

"We did it," I told him. "Those families will be taken care of now."

"*You* did it," he said and kissed me again. "You, the bravest, sweetest girl I've ever met."

"No. You bargained for me. I can't believe you did that."

"I told you. When it came to you or the Outers, I would pick you every time. The good news is that they'll get special consideration now."

I kissed him again, just because he was so sweet. "Guess what I've decided? I'm going to college and becoming an alien rights advocate. I'm going to change the laws, once and for all."

His grin widened. "If anyone can do it, it's you."

At that moment I felt capable of anything. The future was bright with promise, and I planned to live it to the fullest, doing what I could to help those in need. I'd gone from coward to fighter.

"Maybe I'll finally go to college, as well," he said. "Maybe we'll work as a team, fighting for Outers."

"Look out, world," I muttered, and he laughed. Yes, look out, world. I'd finally come into my own and there was no stopping me now.